# SWANN'S
## LAST SONG

# SWANN'S
## LAST SONG

## Charles Salzberg

GREENPOINT PRESS
NEW YORK, NY

*Swann's Last Song* by Charles Salzberg
▪ Second Greenpoint Press Edition, June 2012
▪ First Greenpoint Press Edition, November 2009
▪ Originally published in hardcover by Five Star Mystery, 2008.

This novel is a work of fiction. Names, characters, places and incidents are either the product of the author's imagination, or, if real, used fictitiously.

Permissions to reprint excerpt from *The Instant Enemy* by Ross MacDonald granted by Alfred P. Knopf, a division of Random House, Inc.

ISBN 978-0-9832370-7-5

Library of Congress Cataloging-in-Publication Data

This edition designed by Robert L. Lascaro
LascaroDesign.com
Text set in ITC Stone Serif, Heads set in Helvetica Neue

Greenpoint Press,
a division of New York Writers Resources
PO Box 2062
Lenox Hill Station
New York, N Y 10021

greenpointpress.org

New York Writers Resources:
newyorkwritersresources.com
newyorkwritersworkshop.com
greenpointpress.org
ducts.org

Printed in the United States
on acid-free paper

# Acknowledgments

I'D LIKE TO THANK MY EDITOR, Denise Dietz, for her diligent work on this book, and Matt Harper for believing that someone other than my friends and relatives would actually want to read it; and my agent, Jeff Kleinman, for very much the same reason.

Along the way, many friends, family and colleagues gave their support, including Elliot Ravetz, Mark Goldblatt, Sharyn Wolf, Ross Klavan, Roy Hoffman, Tim Tomlinson, Jonathan Kravetz, Brian Mori, Patty Dann, Janet Kirby, Rusty Jacobs, Doug Garr, Charlie Schulman, Kathryn Gibbs Davis, Caroline Ross, Jessica Hall and P. J. Dempsey. Special thanks to Miranda DeKay, who went well beyond the call of duty in reading this book in manuscript form many more times than any human being should. And to Dana Benningfield for her unwavering support, and to Bob Lascaro for his wonderful design of this book.

Lastly, I'd like to thank all my students, past and present, who taught me far more about the art of writing than they ever imagined they could.

"Things either are what they appear to be; or they are not, nor do they appear to be; or they are, yet do not appear to be; or they are not, and yet appear to be."

—Epiticus

"I had to admit to myself that I lived for nights like these, moving across the city's great broken body, making connections among its millions of cells. I had a crazy wish or fantasy that some day before I died, if I made all the right neural connections, the city would come all the way alive. Like the Bride of Frankenstein."

—Ross MacDonald, *The Instant Enemy*

# NEW YORK

*Swann's office on 156th Streeet and Broadway*

# Rich
# BITCH

I HAVE NO ILLUSIONS LEFT, or at least none that I'm aware of. I had them, like everyone else, but I lost them a long time ago. I don't worry much about abstracts anymore. I try not to ponder too much on the order of the universe, or worry about the nature of man. Philosophy is for college students, bartenders and cab drivers, and I am none of these.

What I am is a skip tracer. A dozen years ago, when I first stumbled into the business, I used to tell people I was in security or maybe, when I was particularly impressed with myself and feeling the least bit romantic, a private investigator. But I got tired of all the questions and the queer looks and inevitable misapprehensions and so, just about the time I lost all my illusions, which unsurprisingly coincided with the death of my wife, I started calling myself what I'd actually turned into—a run-of-the-mill skip tracer, which is nothing more than a glorified collection man. Skip tracer. It made me sound like I worked in a factory, or at some menial, assembly-line job, which is how I felt most of the time. I put in my eight to twelve hours a day, most of it spent casing a car, looking for the best time to pounce, and then either heading home, or making a beeline for the nearest bar, whichever happened to be closer.

That was my life: No delusions, no pride, no romantic notions of what the future might bring, and absolutely no sense of the great adventure of life. But all that was due to change.

I was sitting in my office up on 156th Street and Broadway, right smack in the middle of the poor and huddled masses, which is usually whose business paid the bills.

My feet were propped up on my desk and I was bending a paper clip into all kinds of weird, semi-erotic positions. Frankly, I was far more interested in the flexibility of that particular paper clip than in what my prospective client seated in front of me was saying. She was a middle-aged, burnt-out black woman wearing an ill-fitting curly, auburn wig. Smelling of a mixture of Ajax foaming cleanser and ammonia, wearing an old cloth coat, her stockings rolled up at the knees, she was clutching a black purse and an Associated Food shopping bag filled with essential snack items like Doritos and Slim Jims, a sawed-off black umbrella, and a rumpled copy of the *Daily News*. In short she was, like most of my clients, a woman very familiar with the social-service system of this fine city. She was trying to wheedle me into working for her, but her story was a tired one and, frankly, I was having a little trouble staying awake. Her husband, number three, I think, had just skipped, taking with him the family fortune, consisting of $186, a gold ring—or so she said—and a diamond brooch, which was more likely zirconium. She wanted me to find him. Like I'm some kind of magician. Fact is, I hated those kinds of skip trace numbers. They were a royal pain in the ass. I even preferred repoing cars, which was how I spent most of my time. Cars you find either parked out on the street, or stashed away in some garage. People can be anywhere. They move around. First they're here and then, soon as you shine a light on them, they're gone. And once they disappear they usually don't resurface until they're found lying face down in the gutter with a snoot full of T-bird in their bellies. Or maybe after they've pulled some two-bit, dumb-ass heist and wind up taking a city paid trip out to Rikers Island. Did I have to make a living this way? You bet. Which is why I came up with a rule that unfortunately the majority of us, me included, usually choose to ignore: What's lost is best forgotten.

The pitch was over and now we were getting to the kicker: she wanted to pay me off in food stamps. Can you believe it? Now what the hell was I going to do with a couple hundred bucks worth of orange stamps? Which is exactly why I had that specially printed sign plastered up there on my wall: "Food Stamps Unacceptable As Payment." I got the sign printed up because up here they'll try anything, and this certainly wasn't the first time someone had tried to buy my services with a handful of government stamps. Nor would it be the last. I could just see myself waltzing into the neighborhood bodega and trying to pay for a cup of coffee and a buttered roll with a fistful of those orange stamps. A fine specimen like me. "Hey, cracker," they'd say, "what'sa matter, ain't you got no job? Ha! Ha! Ha!" I would be forced to say something stupid like, "Fuck you, man," and then I'd have to find another place to forage for breakfast.

But then, signs mean nothing to people. They walk when it says "Don't Walk," and they smoke when it says, "Don't Smoke," so naturally they're going to try to pay me off with food stamps when it says "Food Stamps Unacceptable As Payment." But I suppose I shouldn't complain. It's that very human trait, the urge to break the rules, the need to get over on someone, that keeps me in business.

Still, Minnie or Millie, or whatever the hell her name was, was one tough customer. She didn't want to take no for an answer. And so we were well into Round 2 when there was this gentle, almost imperceptible knock at the door. At first I thought maybe it was just the rattle of the pipes, but there it came again.

"Come in," I shouted, over the din of a jackhammer pounding relentlessly outside my window. The door opened slowly and in walked a woman who looked like she just stepped out of the pages of *Vogue* or some other snazzy fashion glossy. She was wearing a gray, fitted suit that stopped just above her knees and black stockings. Figuring she was lost, looking for who knew what, I said, "Something I can do for you?"

"I didn't mean to disturb you," she said. "I have some business I'd like to discuss, but I can certainly wait out in the hall until you're finished."

"That won't be necessary. I'm almost done. Why don't you have a seat?" I gestured toward a ratty old stuffed chair in the corner. She sniffed at it and passed. I couldn't blame her. The chair was something I'd rescued from the street before the Salvation Army could get their hands on it. But I wasn't out to impress anybody. People came to me because they didn't have any other place to go and because, in the end, I usually wound up taking their crummy food stamps. Which is exactly what I agreed to do with Millie, just before I hustled her out of my office with a promise to find her good-for-nothing, globe-trotting husband.

"How can I help you?" I asked, turning to my next victim.

"My husband is missing and I'd like you to find him," she said. La-di-da. Just like that. All business. No tears. No alibis. No sad stories. No long, drawn out prologues. It was as if she'd just misplaced a piece of jewelry and was asking the upstairs maid to take a look for it under the furniture. I couldn't help thinking what a wonderful, wacky world it was where the Millies and a woman like this were both in essentially the same boat.

"Well?" she said. "Yes or no?"

"Maybe we should start at the beginning. Hi," I said, sticking out my hand, "I'm..."

She ignored my hand, rolled her eyes toward the ceiling, and said, "I know who you are, Mr. Swann. What I want to know is are you going to help me?"

I shrugged. "Why come to me? I'm not one to look a gift horse in the mouth, but I'm sure you could have found someone a little more...well, let's just say someone who travels more in the same circles as you do. There are some pretty fancy private detectives in this town. Unfortunately, I'm not one of them."

"I know. But we're not talking about finding me, Mr. Swann," she replied with indisputable logic. "We're talking about finding my husband."

"Well, then, am I to assume your husband is the sort of man who'd be more likely to travel in the same circles as I do?"

"You may assume that he might."

"So you don't send a French poodle out to check the sewers when you can hire a rat."

"Well, Mr. Swann," she said with the slight glimmer of a smile, "I would have thought you'd have a somewhat higher opinion of yourself."

"I do. It's other people's opinions I'm not so sure about. Now, Mrs...?"

"Janus. Sally Janus. So, you'll take the job then."

"That depends."

"On what?"

"Look, you're making me nervous. Why don't you sit down?"

"Must I?"

"Well, my feelings would be hurt if you didn't. You wouldn't want to hurt my feelings, would you?"

She made a face but sat all the same, crossing her very shapely legs. "Mr. Swann, I'm afraid you're making this far more complicated than it need be."

"Look, I don't kid myself. I know who I am. Look around you. This is El Barrio, where they steal the hubcaps off moving cars. I'd like to know what brings you to me and why you're not giving your business to some fancy downtown agency."

"Because I prefer anonymity, Mr. Swann, and no one would ever suspect I hired you. It's as simple as that."

"I doubt it, but I can see a certain logic in what you say," I said. "And who, may I ask, recommended me?"

She laughed. "Oh, let's be serious, Mr. Swann. Who could possibly recommend you to me?"

"You've got a point there. Okay, Mrs. Janus, I'll give it a try. Only I'm not promising anything. These kinds of cases are always tough. Most times husbands who get lost prefer to stay that way."

"Harry was not most husbands. Now, before we go any further, perhaps we ought to discuss money."

"Ah, my favorite subject."

"What are your rates?"

"Pretty much the same as downtown. Three hundred a day plus expenses."

She smiled coyly. She knew I was jacking up my fee, but evidently it didn't matter. That's how much she wanted anonymity. She opened her purse and said, "I suppose I will be subsidizing the redecoration of your office, Mr. Swann."

"Well, frankly, I believe I can make far better use of the money."

"Will two days in advance be sufficient?" she asked, waving a fistful of bills in my face.

"I usually try to get a little more up front...."

"Mr. Swann," she chided me, "may I remind you these are not food stamps...."

"...but you look like you can be trusted."

"How kind," she said, counting out five Benjies, then spreading them out on my desk, as if to dry. "I think we're off on the right track. Trust is very important, don't you think?" she asked, softening her tone somewhat.

"My thoughts exactly. It's what I tell my creditors every day. Now Mrs. Janus, suppose we get down to cases. When did your husband disappear?"

"About a week or so ago."

"It would help if you could be a little more specific about

that. If we're going to get anywhere on this the facts are very important. Lay'em end to end and they make a trail. I follow that trail and then, at the end of it, if I've done my job right, I find what I'm looking for. C follows B which follows A. It's as simple as that."

She looked around the room.

"Something I can get you?" I asked.

"An ashtray, perhaps. I'd hate to soil your lovely floor."

"Sure thing." I removed one from my desk drawer, and when I leaned forward to give it to her I got a good whiff of the perfume she was wearing. She smelled of lilacs, which went a long way in helping get rid of that ammonia and Ajax smell. She took a cigarette from a gold case, lit it with a gold lighter, took a drag, then flicked an ash into the ashtray, all in one smooth, fluid motion.

"Go on," I said, in awe of her dexterity. "You were about to tell me something."

"Well, speaking openly, Mr. Swann, I must admit that Harry and I have a rather unique living arrangement. We're married but apart, if you know what I mean."

"I'm afraid I lead a rather prosaic life, Mrs. Janus, so you'll have to spell things like that out for me." She shot me a look that I charitably took as disdain. "Sorry, but I'm usually working when Oprah comes on."

She let some smoke out of her mouth along with what I took to be a derisive sound. "Harry went his way and I went mine. They call it 'space,' I believe."

"In my day we called it divorce," I muttered.

"He has a small apartment of his own, but he also spends time at our townhouse. So, you see, I can't really say exactly when it was that he disappeared. He might even have been on one of his business trips—he takes a lot of them. I can only tell you the last time I saw him was a week ago Tuesday."

"That's nine days ago. Seems to me that's an awful lot of space. But what with your arrangement and all, what makes you think he's missing?"

"Because even when we were apart he would be in constant touch with me."

"How'd he keep in touch?"

"He calls every day. Like clockwork. Eleven in the morning and six-thirty at night. He's a creature of habit. And I could always reach him through his answering service. I've left messages for almost a week now and he hasn't returned any of my calls. That's not like Harry. And there's something else...." She stopped and sucked on her cigarette, letting smoke escape slowly from between her lips. I watched the wisps of smoke as they rose toward the ceiling then disappeared.

"Yes..."

"He's always been very good about sending money. Every other week, whether he was home or not, I'd get a check via FedEx. I haven't received one for two weeks now. But don't worry, Mr. Swann, you don't have to worry about your fee."

"I'm not worried, Mrs. Janus. I'm guessing that you're the kind of woman who'd have no trouble putting her hands on some cash when she needed it."

She gave me the kind of severe, disapproving look that I hadn't seen since third grade, then continued. "Anyway, Mr. Swann, I brought along a couple of photographs of my husband." She removed two snapshots from her purse and handed them to me. They smelled of the same perfume she was wearing. "I'm afraid they're a few years old."

I examined the photos. One was a shot of a man, from the waist up, standing in front of a building. He was wearing a blue polo shirt and he had a blank look on his face, which sported a short-cropped beard. In the other photo, he was in the middle, surrounded by two beautiful women, one of whom was his wife, the other an attractive redhead whose face was partially obscured by her hair.

"Who's this?"

"I don't know. Some woman we met at this party."

"Just some woman?"

"I never saw her before and I've never seen her since."

"She looks awfully...friendly."

"It was a friendly party. Can we continue?"

"I don't see why not. Can I keep these?"

"I'd like this one of Harry and me—it's the only one I have of us together—but you can keep the other one."

"Nothing more recent, huh?"

"No."

I put it in my pocket. "Why don't you just give me a description."

"Well, he's about fifty."

I'd taken out my notebook and was preparing to write everything down, but I stopped short. "About?"

"I'm sorry, Mr. Swann, but you'll have to bear with me. There are some things I simply don't know for sure."

"This is your husband we're talking about, isn't it?"

"Yes."

"And you don't know his age?"

"That's correct."

"Well, if you don't mind my saying so, Mrs. Janus, that's a little bizarre."

"It is? Well, let's just say that Harry is a very secretive man. I think you'll understand a little better as we go along."

"I hope so. How long have you two been married, or wasn't he there at the time?"

"Seven years and, yes, Mr. Swann, as a matter of fact both of us were present."

"Description?"

"He's five-eleven, with dark brown hair, a hundred and seventy-five pounds, and he has a very small scar just above his right eye." She paused. "I'm afraid I don't know how he got it."

"A duel, no doubt," I mumbled.

"What's that?"

"Nothing."

I was writing all this down, using the shorthand tricks I'd picked up from an old girlfriend. It wasn't the only thing she taught me, just the most useful. "What business is he in?"

She hesitated a moment. "Antiquities. Importing and exporting."

"Where's his office?"

"He doesn't have one. That's why I could only contact him through his answering service—he traveled a lot, you see."

"Okay, give me the number." She did. I wrote it down. "Now what's the address of his apartment?"

Her face was a blank. "The phone number?"

Same thing. I felt this funny, fluttery sensation in the pit of my stomach, like I might be a lot better off finding my previous visitor's husband, who probably wasn't much further away than the local OTB office, but I ignored it. I was beginning to think I might be out of my element here and, for a split second, I contemplated folding up my notebook and calling it a day. But then I took a look at the enormous ring on her finger and thought about the lottery-sized payday I might wring out of her and my greedy little heart skipped a beat. I was trying to think of another semi-intelligent question to ask when I noticed she was impatiently glancing at her watch. Maybe the chauffeur was double-parked downstairs.

"I've got to be going," she said. "My address and phone number are on the back of the photograph. Please call me tomorrow and let me know how you're doing."

"Wait a minute. That's it? That's all you have to tell me?"

"For now, yes."

"Honey, you haven't given me much to go on...."

"It'll have to do. And please, Mr. Swann, don't call me honey."

"Excuse me," I said, appropriately chagrined.

"That's all right," she said charitably.

She got up. I got up too. I walked her to the door. I even opened it for her. "Look," I said. "I don't know how much I can do for you."

She put her hand on mine and moved closer. She smelled

remarkably good. Like an English flower garden. "I'm sure you'll do the very best you can, Mr. Swann. That is what you're getting paid for, isn't it?"

"Yes, that's what I'm getting paid for."

"Call me," she said, and then she was gone.

I went to the window and looked out onto Broadway. It had begun to rain. Mrs. Janus came out of the building, looked around, then stepped out into the street, raised her arm and, out of nowhere, a cab suddenly appeared. She got in and I thought, damn, the rich and beautiful really are different from the rest of us. For one thing, they can always get a cab in New York City when it's raining. ⚐

# The Golden Goose
## GETS LAID TO REST

I DECIDED TO CELEBRATE MY NEWFOUND WEALTH. I could afford to. Bars don't take food stamps, but they do take Benjies. Gladly. And when I had extra dough, which wasn't often, I liked to spread it around. Good for the economy, which could always use a shot in the arm. Besides, I didn't often get the chance to look like a high roller.

Across Broadway is the Paradise Bar and Grill. Mostly, it's a Puerto Rican hangout with a few black regulars tossed in for color. They tolerate the likes of me because every once in a while, just to promote good community relations, I'll buy everyone in the joint a drink. And for that simple act of human kindness the boys at the Paradise sometimes do me the odd favor, like sending me a client or two.

It was only three in the afternoon, but the place was

jumping, mostly with amigos waiting for their old ladies to come home from work and fix dinner, after which they would, no doubt, be right back at the Paradise for the evening's action.

The joint was certainly not on Zagat's list of hip or trendy bars in the city. Far from it, in fact. They hardly ever touched a mop to the floor and it showed. But no one appeared to notice or care. Especially not the roaches, who seemed to appreciate the brand of peanuts Joe Bailey, the owner of the place—a black man who resembled Captain America with his cut physique and chiseled facial features—put out for the paying customers. In fact, one whole wall behind the bar was proudly decorated with Board of Health citations, each one with the city's "Failed" stamp front and center.

In the back there was a pool table and a cigarette machine that only worked when you were nice to it. There was a jukebox up front, but all it played was Tito Puente and various other Puerto Rican favorites, which was exactly what was playing when I strolled in.

"Hey, gringo," Manny the bartender called out as I walked in the door. He's the biggest damn P.R. I've ever seen. Six-four, over three hundred pounds and yet there wasn't an ounce of fat on him. I never knew they grew them so big back in Ponce. On his right arm he had a tattoo of the Puerto Rican flag, in color, that waved when he flexed. Manny was a good fellow to know. He had all sorts of areas of expertise. Need a car heisted and gutted for the insurance? Manny's your man. Success guaranteed. He'd take the car up to the South Bronx or over to the West Side Highway, lift up the hood and the trunk, baptize the insides with a couple of jiggers full of kerosene, toss a match in through the window, and ten minutes later your car would be history, stripped to the bone, burned nearly beyond recognition, with Allstate's friendly fist knocking at your door. Or, if you needed a green card and didn't feel like marrying just any old *chica*, Manny knows the guy who can confer instant citizenship on your ass.

"Long time no see," said Manny, as he dunked dirty glasses

into a tub of soapy water. He hardly kept them in there long enough to do any real damage to the faintest-hearted bacteria, but his heart was in the right place.

"I been pretty busy," I said, digging into my pocket for one of the bills. I put it on the bar, smoothed it out, and said, "Look, Manny, you give me twenty back, lay two shots of Johnny Walker Black on me, the real stuff, then use the rest to buy all my friends here a drink."

Manny smiled, winked, scoffed up the fifty with one of his over-sized meat hooks and replaced it with a wrinkled ten and two fives, one with a corner missing. He poured my drinks and then started to see to the others.

For over a year now the Paradise Bar and Grill had been a second home to me. It was there when I needed it. It was there when no one else was. It was there when my wife died in a freak accident, one of those items you read under a ridiculously large headline on the front page of the *New York Post*. She was walking down the street minding her own business when a manhole cover exploded. Like a runaway Frisbee it flew through the air and when it got close to earth she happened to be in its path. When it hit her it virtually cut her in half and she bled to death before the ambulance even arrived. All this just because she was in the wrong place at the wrong time. It was so bizarre, so unbelievable, that people, when I tell them, and that's only when I'm drunk enough not to remember to keep it to myself, think I'm making it up. I'm not. I couldn't. I'm just not that imaginative. Sometimes they even remember the story in the papers, which makes it worse, making my wife part of tabloid history, along with Headless Body in Topless Bar. And to this day, every time I walk in the street and see steam coming from one of those manhole covers, I can't help but shudder and cross quickly to the other side of the street, as visions of a flying disc of steel careen through my head.

After it happened I went through a very bad period, which culminated in a brief stay at a hospital. All this did little to help the kid we had, who was five at the time. I tried to pull myself back together but it wasn't easy. I would be okay for a while and then, out of the blue, I'd start crying. It scared me. It scared my son. In order to save him—and maybe myself—I had to send him off to live with my wife's folks in Missouri. It was better that way. I see him a few times a year and feel guilty about it, which is the way it's supposed to be. I talk to him a couple times a week, sometimes less. Every time I see him he's a different person. He knows more. He's bigger. I suppose, if I had to, I could pick him out of a crowd, but I have to admit, if I'm honest with myself, that it wouldn't be easy. I feel myself growing older through him and then I feel even more alone. The Paradise Bar and Grill helps me get over that alone feeling. Nothing helps me with the growing old part.

I hung around the Paradise Bar and Grill for half an hour or so, until my drinks were gone and I couldn't take any more of the good will I'd generated, or the pats on the back, which were beginning to take their toll. I started to leave, but before I got far one of the regulars, a pimply-faced punk named Billy D., who spent half his childhood in the Bronx House of Detention where he learned all sorts of useful vocational skills like how to open parking meters with a nail file, called out, "Hey, Swann, how about some po-it-tree, man?"

Once, just once, you get a little snookered and start reciting a bit of harmless poetry you once memorized in a moment of weakness and you're a marked man for life.

"Sorry, Billy D." I said. "I've got work to do. Some other time, maybe."

But they were feeling real good over at the Paradise Bar and Grill, thanks to me, I might add, so they were not about to take no for an answer.

"Come on, Swannee," Manny purred sweetly from behind the bar, as the Puerto Rican flag waved high. "It won't take long, man."

When Manny made a personal appeal like that, I found

it nigh unto impossible to resist. He was not the sort of guy you'd want mad at you. I'd seen him in action. He threw three wise guys out of the joint one night without even working up a sweat.

"Just one," I said, and I began:

*Adam was my grandfather,*
*A tall, spoiled child.*
*A red clay tower*
*In Eden, green and mild.*
*He ripped the Sinful Pippin*
*From its sanctimonious limb.*
*Adam was my grandfather*
*And I take after him.*
*Noah was my uncle*
*And he got dead drunk.*
*There were planets in his liquor can*
*And lizards in his bunk....*

At this point in my narrative, the patrons of the Paradise Bar and Grill began to roar with laughter. They cheered. They threw peanuts around the room. They sloshed beer out of their mugs. They stood up and raised their glasses. They toasted me. They toasted Noah and his beer cans. They toasted lizards and other slimy reptiles. They toasted Manny. They toasted Joe Bailey. They toasted every fucking P.R. fighter in the whole town. They even toasted the goddamn mayor and half of them didn't even know who the hell he was. And so, with all this toasting going on, I took the opportunity to slip out, knowing full well the next time I showed my white ass in the Paradise Bar and Grill I'd better be prepared to buy a few rounds and recite "The Charge of the Light Brigade" from start to finish.

I went back upstairs to my office to start the ball rolling with a few key phone calls.

The first and, as it turned out, the only call I had to make was to an acquaintance in the police department, Detective John Kelly. I first ran into him when I was arrested for grand theft auto. The charges were dropped when they found I was only repossessing a car for delinquent payments. I gave him Janus's description, what little I had, without giving him the name, then twiddled my thumbs while waiting to find out if they had any reports on anyone who might fit the bill. Five minutes later, Kelly was back on the line.

"What's the guy's name, Swann?"

"I'm afraid I can't say right now."

"How you expect me to help if I don't got the name?"

"Description should do for now."

"Why you looking for this guy?"

"The rent's due. He took a powder and his wife's looking for him. I'm just the hired help. You know something or not?"

"I think maybe you ought to get down here. We got things to talk about."

"Like what?"

"Just get your ass down here."

I was on an expense account, so I took a cab. It made me feel like I could live the way I couldn't. Of course, it took me a lot longer to get one than it did the Janus woman, but that was to be expected. The handwritten receipt—the printer on the meter was broken, big surprise—was for $9.50. I added a discreet 1 in front of the 9. She could afford it and who knew how long I'd be on the case. For all I knew the next day I could be spending my time trying to unload a handful of food stamps on the black market.

I was ushered into Kelly's puke-green office by his partner, the redoubtable Detective Patterson. He took a seat in the corner, while I made myself as comfortable as possible in a hard-backed folding chair in front of Kelly's desk.

"Well?" I said.

Kelly ignored me, shifting around some papers on his desk. Finally, he leaned back in his chair, sucking on a big cigar, smiled and said, "I think maybe we got something here, Swann...." It could be that sometimes a cigar is just a cigar, but with Kelly I don't think so. He's a big man, almost as big as Manny but with none of Manny's redeeming qualities. I kept hoping maybe he'd topple over, land on his head, and then we'd all get a good laugh.

"Yeah?"

"Yeah. But first I want the guy's name."

"First you tell me something, then I'll be glad to give you the name."

"Jesus fucking Christ!" Kelly roared, as he rose quickly, sending his chair flying backward into the wall.

"Easy, Kelly, easy," the detective's partner, Patterson, warned, as he sat in the corner cleaning his fingernails with a pocketknife.

"I thought I told you to cut that out," Kelly said, staring coldly at his partner.

"Cut what out?" Patterson asked, feigning ignorance. He just loved getting under Kelly's skin. And he knew just how to do it, too.

"You know what the hell I'm talking about. That friggin' digging around under your nails. It don't matter how much you dig, Patterson, it still looks like you been shoveling shit all day. Why the hell don't you try wearing gloves if you're so damn worried about how your friggin' hands look."

"Ever hear about cleanliness being next to godliness, Kelly?" Patterson shot back.

"You work in shit, you look like shit," Kelly answered, and the issue died there, at least for the moment, as Kelly turned his attention to me.

"All right, Swann, we had a killing the other day and the guy happens to fit the description you gave us...."

"The killer?"

"Nope."

"You're sure?"

"Yup."

"Scar, too?"

"Well, we got a slight problem there. The victim was zapped three times in the head, so his face wasn't in no condition to check for scars."

"Whew," I whistled, thinking if it was Janus then my gravy train had come to the end of the line. I don't want to sound like I haven't got a heart, but the truth is I didn't know the guy, and it wasn't like his wife and he were about to present any heavy competition to Tristan and Isolde.

"We checked his prints, but they're not on file anywhere," said Patterson. "We'll check the dental files and do some other testing, but that'll take some time.

"So, what's his name, Swann?" Kelly asked, as he lumbered around the small room like the big, ugly bear he was. His gut, sagging over his belt buckle, shook comically as he moved. He was wearing baggy, brown slacks, a pair of black, orthopedic space shoes that almost made me feel sorry for him—almost—a white button-down shirt rolled up at the sleeves—his jacket hung limply from a coat rack in the corner—and he sported a shoulder holster which, because of the tightness with which it was strapped across his chest, hindered any possibility of fluid motion, making him look as if he were wearing a harness.

"Harry Janus."

"Where's he live?"

"Don't know."

"Don't get cute," Kelly bellowed, his jowly red face turning a deep crimson, his body shaking with rage.

"Hey, Kelly, better watch it or you'll give yourself a heart attack," his partner warned, still calmly attacking his fingernails, though by this time he'd changed weapons and was using a bent paper clip.

Kelly glared at his partner. "Shut up, Patterson. When I need a health report from you, I'll ask for it. Now, Swann, you tell me where the fuck the guy lived or I'm gonna throw your wise ass in the can and it's very possible you ain't never gonna see the light of day."

"You seem to forget, Kelly, that I was looking for the guy. If I knew where he lived then I'd have known where to find him, wouldn't I?"

"That don't make no sense. He wasn't where he lived when we found him."

"Oh, yeah? Where was he?"

"None of your damn business. Now who hired you? And don't give me none of that confidentiality crap. This is a murder investigation."

"And I'm a cooperative citizen. Listen, I was paid to find the guy and if this is him that's just what I did. His wife was the one who hired me. Her address is..." I took out the photo and read from the back of it. "Two-twenty-five East 70th Street. The name's Sally Janus."

Kelly took it down on a piece of paper. "Okay, that's all for now. You can go."

"Not so fast. Tell me what happened."

Kelly smiled and tapped his pencil against the side of his desk. "What do I look like, Swann, *The New York Times*?"

"Come on, Kelly, give me a break, will you?" He grinned even wider. He liked having me at his mercy.

"We found him in some Times Square sleaze house with his brains scattered all over the walls. We figure he was taken off by some pimp who was just out for a quick score. He was well dressed and he didn't look like he had no business there. No identification on him. The labels were torn out of his clothes. That's about the size of it."

"Doesn't sound like the sort of place a guy like Janus would be hanging out," I said, though I remembered his wife had hinted at something out of the ordinary. After all, she hired me, didn't she? "Well, it's none of my business anymore. I've done what I was paid to do. You going to notify the wife?"

"Yeah. You're off the case, Swann. Hope you got your dough

upfront, pal, because people don't like shelling out for damaged goods. Unless, of course, this ain't the guy. Then you're right back where you started from, aren't you?

"Guess so."

"But for now, at least, you can go back to hot-wiring jalopies."

"You're a sweetheart, Kelly."

OUTSIDE, THE RAIN HAD BEGUN TO FALL AGAIN. It was only five o'clock, but already it was dark and the streets were illuminated only by car headlights and the glowing street lamps reflecting off the wet pavement. I took the subway back up to my office, but forged a receipt anyway. I figured if the job was over, the least I could do was to get an extra seventeen bucks out of it.

I mailed my bill out the next day when I read in the *Daily News*, page 25, that the body found in the Metropolitan Hotel three days before belonged to one "Harry Janus, businessman."

Three days later, in an envelope that smelled faintly of lilacs, I received a check for $35 and change—my expenses. There was no note. I thought the least she could have done was thank me. After all, I did find her husband, didn't I? ⚸

# Same Old
## SAME OLD

A FEW DAYS LATER, I found myself in a very familiar
position: leaning against the side of an Upper East Side
apartment building, a prop newspaper in my hands.

I was on the job.

It works like this: Man sees a commercial on TV for a
very cool, very sleek, very desirable looking car. Man pictures
himself in the driver's seat of that very same car perhaps with
a very cool, very sleek, very desirable looking woman, flowing
blond hair, tight-fitting dress, sitting next to him. Man says to
himself, "Hey, why shouldn't I be driving that sweet machine,
sitting next to that gorgeous babe?" Does it occur to him that
the reason that maybe he ought not be driving that "sweet
machine" and sitting next to that gorgeous looking babe is that
(a) he doesn't have the money to pay for it, and (b) credit can
be a very dangerous thing? Absolutely not.

This is America, bud. A chicken in every pot. A car in every garage, whether you've got a garage or not. And so, with very little or even nothing down, and an exorbitant amount to be repaid each month, every red-blooded American can own his or her own dream machine. But be forewarned, if you miss a few payments that dream can turn into a nightmare. And that's where I come in. I am not the dream catcher, but rather think of me as the dream snatcher. It is a dirty job, but someone has to do it. Unfortunately, that night that someone was me.

It was nearly sundown and when it would finally get dark enough for me to be just another anonymous man on the street, I would spring into action.

I checked my watch. 7:15. Sunset was officially 7:18. At approximately 7:24, there would be a burst of light, like the explosion of the flame on a candle before finally going out, the last gasp of daylight, and then it would be dark, dark enough for vampires and werewolves and dark enough for me to do the deed for which I was to be paid.

I had arrived almost an hour and a half earlier, just in time to post myself in a strategic position in front of the apartment building where my mark resided. I waited for him to get home—recognizing him from a photograph provided by the finance company—and then I canvassed the neighborhood to see where he had parked his car, a black Lexus. You would think that someone who owned a car like that could afford a garage but, fortunately for me, this wasn't the case. Garages were a tougher nut to crack. It usually meant dough changing hands, and the more people you had involved in a transaction like this the better chance there was of it going belly up.

7:24. The burst of light. Then, as if a light switch dimmer had been dialed down, darkness fell seemingly all at once. Along with the darkness came the butterflies I began to feel flapping around in my stomach. This was not unusual. No matter how many times I did this, I was still nervous every time. Would I get caught by the owner of the car, and would I find myself on the wrong end of a baseball bat? Would some nosy bystander call the cops and cause me all kinds of red tape problems? Yeah, maybe it was those things. But maybe it was also that in too many ways I actually identified with the person whose car I was taking and not with the finance company that was paying my salary. How would I like it if someone showed up in the dead of night and took something I valued, something I'd staked my identity on? Isn't that sort of what happened to my life when my wife was killed and I had to give up my son?

Some people get a rush from repoing a car. Like a shot of adrenaline mainlined into a vein. Not me. And some skip tracers actually like to see the shock and surprise of the soon-to-be-former owner when he sees his dreamboat burning rubber without him in the driver's seat. In fact, I once knew a guy, one of the best, who would take the car and then come back the next morning just so he could see the look on the owner's face when he came out of his house expecting to see his automobile sitting there where he'd parked it.

Not me. My *modus operandi* was to take the car as quickly and as unobtrusively as possible and then fade silently into the night. That was the way I planned it, but it wasn't always the way it worked out.

7:30. Darkness. I tossed the newspaper into the nearest trash can and headed toward the Lexus. With every step, my heartbeat thumped quicker and louder in my chest. I jammed my hands into my pockets to stop them from shaking. Yes, I'd done this a hundred times before, but it didn't matter. I was just as nervous as the first time. Maybe even more.

I was in a residential neighborhood and the sidewalks were fairly empty, most people in their homes for the evening, doing the kinds of normal things I could only dream of doing: having dinner with their families; playing with their children; watching "Entertainment Tonight" or "Jeopardy." I took a look around. A young couple was walking toward me, arm in arm, engrossed in each other's conversation. I stepped toward a store window and looked inside. I could see the couple pass in the reflection in the window. When they'd cleared the area, I stepped toward the car as I pulled the gizmo out of my pocket that would pop the lock and let me in. I bent down toward the door handle trying to make it look as if I were just another owner moving his car. I inserted the long, thin tool into the lock and twisted. I heard a pop. So far, so good. I opened the door and slid into the front seat. In adjusting the rearview mirror I saw a man and a woman walking slowly toward me. I looked closer. Dammit! It was the owner of the car. He hadn't seen me yet, nor had he noticed that anyone was in his beloved car, but he would soon enough. I fumbled with the ignition key I had been provided, trying to aim it in the right direction. I launched into my mantra. "Plenty of time. Plenty of time..."

With one eye still riveted to the rearview mirror, my hand shaking, I touched the front edge of the key to the ignition. I saw the man look up, in the direction of his car. For a split second, our eyes seemed to meet and I was frozen in time.

The man stopped dead in his tracks. I could see a look of confusion on his face and I could see words start to form on his lips. I turned the key, praying the engine would roll over. Out of the corner of my eye, I saw the man say something to the woman standing next to him and then he started running toward me, waving his arms, screaming, "Hey, that's my car! What the fuck is going on?"

The sound of the engine filled the air. I put it in reverse, eased my foot onto the gas, backed up a few feet, then cranked it into forward, hit the gas and took off. By this time, the owner had reached the curb where his car had formerly resided. He shook his fist as more curses flew from his mouth. I trained my eyes ahead and then, suddenly, I heard a crashing sound and then a splat coming from behind me. I looked back and saw that the back window had been smashed—there was a trash can lying in the street. I glanced into the rearview mirror and saw the owner chasing me out into the street. Suddenly, he stopped and went into a throwing motion. I gunned the engine as I saw an empty soda can clunk harmlessly to the ground behind the car, which was now safely turning the corner, headed in the direction of the garage where I was to deliver it. ⚡

# Back in The Saddle
## AGAIN

SOME PEOPLE WILL DO ANYTHING FOR MONEY. I am one of those people. After all, it is my heritage. I am an American, from the tip of my wallet to the bottom of my bank account. I am just one more in a long line of great Americans: John D. Rockefeller, Henry Ford, Jay Gould, Andrew Carnegie and Bill Gates. They are my fathers; I am their son....

So, it shouldn't be surprising that I jumped at the opportunity to take more money from Sally Janus.

The next morning, I was sitting in my office working, or rather trying to work, the *New York Times* crossword puzzle while waiting for my next welfare case to darken my door, when I got a call from Mrs. Janus. She wanted to see me. I could practically smell the lilacs over the phone, so I said I'd be right over.

I took the bus downtown. No expense account, you understand. Anyway, sometimes a fellow likes to travel slowly and see where he's going as well as where he's been.

The Janus townhouse was located on a well-kept, tree-lined block just off Park Avenue. It was painted bright yellow with blue trim around the windows, which were framed with fire-engine-red shutters, all of which seemed calculated to make it stand out from the other relatively drab brown and gray townhouses on the block.

The doorknob was solid, hand-sculpted brass, with the head of a lion serving as the knocker. I slid my hand into the lion's mouth and rapped three times. A moment later there was Mrs. Janus, dressed in a pair of tight-fitting blue jeans, appropriately faded, and a black tee-shirt with SALLY printed boldly across the front in large, sparkling silver letters. Below was a large, red apple with a bite taken out of it.

"Come in, Mr. Swann," she purred in a manner light years away from the one she'd exhibited a mere two weeks earlier. She opened the door just wide enough for me to enter.

I looked closely at her face. Either she wasn't wearing any makeup or she was so skilled at applying it that it just looked that way. This morning her eyes were a bright blue, matching the color of the sky.

She guided me into the living room, a room flashing with chrome, Lucite and glass, with well-cushioned chairs that tilted, turned and rocked. A virtual Disneyland of furniture. On the walls were several paintings that looked as if they belonged in a museum. In one corner there was a large, blindingly white grand piano with several framed photographs on top. One entire wall was occupied by a bookcase, entirely filled with hardcover books.

Mrs. Janus took a seat on the sofa. She left plenty of room for me to sit beside her, but instead I chose a chair facing her.

"So, what's up?" I asked.

"I'd like to hire you again," she said, crossing her legs.

"Because I did such a bang-up job the last time, I suppose."

"I don't think that's anything to joke about."

"You're right. I'm sorry. And I'm sorry about your loss."

"I'm sure you are."

"Actually, I'm sorry about everyone's loss. Maybe that's why I do what I do."

She lowered her eyes. "And I'm sorry. I shouldn't take that tone with you. It's not your fault my husband's dead. But I would like you find out who murdered him."

I started to laugh, then stopped myself. "I'm afraid you've got me mixed up with somebody else. I don't do those kinds of things—finding cars and errant spouses is my bag. Besides, though I hate to fall victim to clichés, the cops are paid to take care of things like that."

"But I'm willing to pay you," she said. She'd now taken to slowly running her hand through her hair. I watched her. How could I help it? I knew she was doing it to get what she wanted from me and I also knew it was having the desired effect. She had beautiful hands. Long, lovely fingers, with long, well-manicured fingernails painted a light shade of pink. The light from beside the sofa made her nails shine brightly. She'd been out in the sun recently and her hands were tanned a light brown, as was her face.

"Pay me for what? The cops know how and why your husband was killed. Now it's just a simple matter of picking up the right guy. I'm not trained for that sort of thing. Fact is, I'm trained for very little."

She placed both hands together, fingers to fingers, then collapsed them, making a hollow dome out of her hands. "They're wrong," she said softly. "Harry was not killed the way they say he was."

"How's that?"

"Because he just wasn't, that's all."

Logic like that is irrefutable. Nevertheless, I was doing all I could to resist the temptation of money and whatever else

Mrs. Janus might be offering. There was something about this woman that puzzled me. Something just didn't fit, besides me being in that apartment, I mean. I kept sensing there was more to the situation than what I was being told. I don't always trust my instincts because every time I do I wind up making a fool of myself, but this time, well, I wondered if maybe this was the exception that might prove the rule. I wanted to know why she wanted me to find her husband's killer, why she didn't trust the police, why it mattered, so I asked.

She didn't answer right away. Instead, she reached for a silver cigarette box on the coffee table, initials SJH, took a cigarette, and flicked her lighter. She drew on it slowly, then exhaled a long, heavy stream of smoke. When it settled there like a cloud in front of her face, she finally answered.

"Maybe I'm afraid."

"Afraid of what?"

"Afraid someone will come after me, too."

"And why should that be?"

"I don't know, but wouldn't you be worried? I know Harry didn't die the way they said. He wasn't the kind of person you'd find in a place like that."

I didn't want to argue with her. I just wanted to get out of there. Money, when it's someone else's, makes me nervous. And there was something about this woman that increased my nerves twofold.

"You ought to tell the cops about your misgivings." I started to get up, but she reached across and put her hand on my arm.

"Mr. Swann, you must understand that this is very important to me. I must find out who killed Harry and why." Suddenly, the hard edge to her voice disappeared. Was this just another form of manipulation to get what she wanted?

"I'm willing to pay you, Mr. Swann," she said, sounding even more desperate. "Very handsomely, in fact."

"You already said that."

"I know, but I thought it was important."

"Well, I suppose it is."

"I'd even be willing to up your daily rate. How does $350 sound?"

"Very tempting."

"And I would be willing to pay you one week in advance. And, if you didn't make any progress in that time, well, we could just end our association right there."

How could I turn down an offer like that? I figured the cops probably knew what they were doing and that Janus was killed just the way they said. But if this whacked-out widow wanted to pay me $350 a day just to tell her that, well, that was her business.

"Okay," I said. "You've got yourself a deal."

She smiled, leaned over and kissed me on the cheek. Lilacs went right up my nose. "I'll write you a check," she said, "if that's all right."

"Sure," I said. Dorothy, one of the regular tellers at my bank, would probably keel over when she saw it. Usually my deposits run around fifty bucks and my checks smell of *cuchifritos*, not lilacs.

"All right," I said, "let's get started. Tell me what you know about your late husband and his habits."

"I met Harry seven years ago at a cocktail party. I was used to guys coming on to me, but he was different. I'd say he was charming, but it was more than that. He seemed... so interested. He looked me right in the eye all the time we were talking. He didn't use those ridiculous lines men use all the time. He asked me questions. And he listened to the answers. Then he asked more questions. I wound up telling him things I'd never told anyone before, much less a virtual stranger. And physically, he knew just when to touch me...and how. He was smart, too, but he didn't flaunt it. I was completely captivated. He asked me out—if he hadn't, I probably would have asked him. He was the smartest man I'd ever met. He knew something about everything. He was well-traveled. He knew all the right people.

Three weeks later he asked me to marry him. I didn't have to think twice. He was like someone you talk about with your friends but don't ever believe you'll meet. Maybe you don't even believe there is such a person alive. It was as if he knew just what I was looking for and gave it to me, only it wasn't anything artificial. That's just the way he was. He was like that with everyone. People liked Harry; they gravitated to him. They wanted him to like them...."

I was skeptical. I had an uncle like that who, it wound up, used to beat the hell out of his wife and kids.

"From the beginning he was always taking these business trips. He'd be away for a few days, sometimes a week, but he called every day and made sure there was a way to reach him in an emergency."

"And when did this 'space' thing develop?"

"It wasn't anything planned, it just happened and because of it our time spent together was that much better. I never doubted for a moment that he loved me."

"Anyone else he loved?"

She glared at me. "He didn't cheat on me, if that's what you're asking."

That was exactly what I was asking and that was exactly the answer I'd expected. But that didn't mean it was the truth. But there was no use beating that dead horse, so I moved on.

"What about before you met him?"

"What do you mean?"

"I mean, what was his life like then?"

She shrugged.

"You never talked about it?"

"No."

"You never asked?"

"Maybe it was the mystery that kept me attracted."

This was something I couldn't quite get my head around. To me, mysteries are there to be solved. I hate loose ends. I hate unanswered questions. Maybe that's why I don't have any friends—except the guys at the P B & G, that is—because I ask too many damn questions and I want all the answers. Without them, I feel incomplete, ineffective, like I'm floating in mid-air. It's not a feeling I like.

"What about family? Where did he come from?"

"He never mentioned any family. I assumed they were dead. I think he spent some time out west. California, maybe. But I don't think he was born there. Europe, Germany, maybe."

"What makes you think it was Germany?"

"Oh, I don't know. It was just an impression I had. I once saw some business papers on his desk and they were in German. I assumed that he could speak the language, so it makes sense that he spent time there, at the very least."

"How about friends?"

"Everybody he met was a friend, but there was no one he hung out with regularly, if that's what you mean."

"Doesn't that strike you as a little odd?"

"You had to know Harry. He always told me I was all he needed, and I didn't really want to share him with anybody else. Besides, he was always involved in one business project or another."

"Okay, let's get back to other women."

"I told you, there were no other women. Look, Swann, this is not a divorce action I'm hiring you for."

"You don't think he wound up in that sleazy hotel because he was looking for the Disney store, do you?"

She was silent.

"Listen, it's part of my job to ask these kinds of questions. If you don't like it, you can find somebody else who'll take every thing on faith."

"If you want to pursue that avenue, that's your business. But I think you'll find it fruitless."

"Jealousy makes people do strange things."

"What's that supposed to mean?"

"A man who plays in the field sometimes gets stung by

bees." I stared at her and could see that she wasn't about to budge. I made a mental note: *cherchez la femme.* "Okay, you think not, then I'll concentrate in other areas for now. How about showing me his room."

I followed her up the stairs. I paused for a moment on the second floor, as she started up to the third.

"What's here?" I asked, half out of curiosity, half to catch my breath.

"The den, library, and a small guest room."

"Don't suppose you had many guests."

She smiled, then continued climbing.

The bedrooms were on the third floor. "This one's mine," she said, pointing to a room on the right. "And this was Harry's," she added, gesturing toward one at the other end of the hall.

"Ladies first," I said, gesturing toward her husband's room.

There was a bed, a fancy dresser, a floor lamp, a chair, and a night table with a telephone, small lamp, clock radio and address book on it. A mirror hung over the dresser and a print of a painting by Van Gogh—a pair of empty work boots—hung from the wall at one end of the bed.

"Kind of sparse, isn't it?"

"That's the way he liked it. This was more like a...well, he'd come in here if he got home late and didn't want to wake me. Or if he got up in the middle of the night and decided to do a little work." She sat at the edge of the bed while I searched the closet. A few suits, a couple of sport jackets, a half dozen shirts, that's all. I turned out the pockets. Nothing. Not even a matchbook cover.

"Some of his things are in the other room," she explained. "I haven't had a chance to get rid of them yet. I don't know what to do with them. If any fit, you're welcome to them."

The idea of wearing a dead man's clothes gave me the creeps. "No thanks," I said. I picked up the dead man's address book and thumbed through it.

"The police have already checked that," she said. "There

isn't much there. Mostly neighborhood places—laundry, dry cleaner, like that. Harry carried his personal address book with him all the time."

"Oh yeah? Where is it now?"

"I don't know."

"Did the cops find it?"

"If they did they didn't tell me about it."

"What about a computer? Did he have one?"

"No. He didn't believe in them. He kept every thing up here." She tapped the side of her head.

"Everything?"

"Well, there's a filing cabinet down in the basement."

"I'll check it before I leave."

I pulled out the night table drawer, but it slid from its grooves and a small piece of paper fell to the floor. I stooped to pick it up.

"What is it?" Sally Janus asked.

"Looks like the return address from a letter. It must have been wedged behind the drawer." I handed it to her. She read aloud, "Carole Cheney, 22256½ Chandler Boulevard."

"Mean anything to you."

"No, I'm afraid not."

I retrieved the paper and stuffed it in my pocket.

Sally Janus sat back down on the edge of the bed, crossed her legs and fidgeted with her hands, while I checked the rest of the room. I pulled out other drawers, looked under the bed, checked beneath the mattress. Nothing. When I'd finished I looked back at Sally Janus, who was staring blankly at the wall, squeezing her hands together. Her breasts heaved up and down rhythmically as she breathed, punctuating her black tee-shirt just below the S and Y of her name. I sat down beside her. I assumed she was wondering who the woman on the envelope was. I touched her shoulder lightly and she jumped, startled.

"You all right?"

"Uh-huh," she said. I noticed the color of her eyes had

changed to a light shade of blue-green.

"You sure?"

"Yes."

"Well, I think I ought to take a look down in the basement and then head out and begin to earn my salary."

Before going down to the basement, I made a detour to the library, where I checked out the titles of some of the books on his shelves. There were a few novels, authors like Saul Bellow, Philip Roth, Nabokov, Hemingway and Fitzgerald—a bunch of biographies: Winston Churchill, FDR—an unusual number of books about World War II, a biography of Adolph Hitler, Shirer's *The Rise and Fall of the Third Reich*—and a few books about anthropology, including works by Louis Leakey and Jane Goodall. There was also a shelf of books devoted to art, with several catalogues from auction houses like Christie's and Sotheby's. I pulled out a couple and thumbed through them.

"Your husband had very eclectic tastes."

"He liked to read."

I pulled out Leakey's autobiography, *White African*. From the shape of the spine, I could see that it had obviously been read several times.

"A favorite of his?"

"I don't really know. He liked to come in here to read…or, late at night, so he didn't disturb me."

"A very considerate man," I said, as I returned the book to its place on the shelf.

"He seemed to have a particular interest in art."

"Yes," she said curtly, and for some reason I could see that it wasn't a subject she wanted me to pursue so, of course, that's exactly what I did.

"I noticed those paintings in your living room. They aren't knockoffs, are they?"

"No, they aren't."

"Did he deal in art?"

"Not really."

"But he liked to buy it?"

"I think those were gifts from business contacts."

"Nice gifts."

"I think you said you'd like to see what's in the basement."

I moved down to the basement, which smelled slightly of sewer gas. It was, in stark contrast to the rest of the house, dark, dank and messy. I flicked on the light and looked around. I spotted a three-drawer black cabinet near a back wall. I tried to open it, but it was locked, so I used my handy Swiss Army knife to pry it open. Most of what was there was business papers, lists of items like vases and figurines, along with a few photographs of small statues and what looked like primitive art. There was a folder labeled travel receipts. I opened it up and thumbed through it. The receipt portion of a first-class, roundtrip ticket from New York to L.A., dated only ten days earlier, just a couple of days before Janus was murdered, caught my eye. But the ticket was made out not to Harry Janus, but to Hugh Jenner. Harry Janus. Hugh Jenner. Same initials. And since it was to L.A., maybe it was connected to this Carole Cheney woman. I folded the receipt and tucked it in my pocket.

When I got back upstairs, Sally Janus was in the living room, talking on the phone. When she saw me, she hung up quickly.

"Find anything?" she asked.

"Not much. There might be something of interest down there, but I won't know what it is until I do some more legwork. Your husband did some importing, didn't he?"

"Yes, that was one of his businesses. Do you think it could have anything to do with his murder?"

I shrugged.

"So, what's next? Where will you begin?"

I thought for a moment. "Where you always begin in cases like this."

"Where's that?"

"The scene of the crime, of course." 🕇

# Crime and
# PUNISHMENT

B Y THE TIME I LEFT THE JANUS TOWNHOUSE the weather had changed, as several fair weather clouds played hide and seek with the sun. The quickest way to the Metropolitan Hotel was by subway. Also the cheapest. Week in advance or no, I could always use the extra dough, so I took the train and charged for a cab. I didn't feel the least bit guilty. Sally Janus, a rich widow now, could afford it.

I paced nervously back and forth across the deserted subway platform, waiting for the train to arrive. I thought about what I'd gotten myself into. In the best of all possible worlds, the cops would pick up the killer in a few days and I'd be a couple grand richer. But guys like me, born with the taste of copper, not silver, in their mouths, usually have to earn their money. That's just the way it was. I've never had a job that looked easy turn out that way…and I didn't think this was going to be any different.

I looked at my watch. It seemed I'd been down there hours instead of minutes. When I looked up I noticed a fellow in a trench coat, leaning against a pole, reading the newspaper. As soon as we made momentary eye contact, he turned away, as if looking down the tunnel for the arrival of the train. Just then, a breeze started blowing up, signaling the imminent arrival of the subway.

When I got off the train, I headed west. I'd walked only a few blocks crosstown when I stopped to tie my shoelace, bracing my foot on a fire hydrant. It was then that I saw the guy from the subway behind me. When he saw me look up, he quickly looked away and turned to face a store window. I was being followed. I'd done enough of it myself to know the drill.

In an attempt to lose him, I ducked into the nearest building, took the elevator up to the fourth floor, walked down one floor, then took the elevator back to the lobby. I then walked all the way over to Ninth Avenue, then back east toward Eighth. By this time, I figured I'd lost him.

The Metropolitan Hotel, with the t and the l missing from the sign, was a slim, eight-story building with paint peeling and chunks of concrete missing from the decaying facade. The area was in the midst of being Disneyfied, and already the two buildings that flanked it were boarded up, just waiting for the demolition ball to hit.

Squinting through a thick haze of cigarette smoke—at least I hoped that's what it was—I made my way up to the front desk, where I faced a bald, heavy-set desk clerk. I asked him about the room where Harry Janus was iced. Ten bucks later he handed me the key.

A hand-printed sign announced that the elevator was "busted," so I took the stairs, which smelled of urine, suddenly making me homesick for the barrio. When I reached the fourth floor, I opened the stairway door onto a dimly lit hallway about forty feet long. The silence was eerie. It was as if I were the only one in the place. I stopped and listened for a minute, half hoping for some signs of life. Nothing. I forged ahead. When I reached the room, I slipped the key into the lock. It was jammed. I twisted the knob, gave the door a good push, and it opened. So much for security.

It was dark inside. The shades were drawn. I felt along the wall for the light switch and flipped it on. The room became lit only by one bare bulb swaying gently from the middle of the ceiling. A couple of roaches skittered across the floor and found safety inside the walls.

The room was small, airless and reeked of a foul, sour odor, like  urine, though I didn't want to imagine that particular scenario. It was sparsely furnished with a bed, dresser and a small table next to the bed. There was a bathroom to the left and a small closet to the right.

I don't know what I expected to find after a horde of cops had traipsed through the room, but I looked around anyway. Glancing down at the floor I could still make out the faint chalk lines that marked the position of Janus's body when it was found. I knelt down and found traces of dried blood within the outline and, on the wall, there was a small area discolored by blood.

I checked the closet. Empty. So was the night table. I stood around for a moment, my hands on my hips, wondering what the hell I was doing there. I felt like an imposter. What did I expect to find? A clue that the cops somehow missed? And what would I know about clues to a murder anyway? I wasn't trained for this. I wasn't trained for much of anything, in fact. Two years of college, most of which I slept through. Then a couple of years of menial jobs trying to find myself. The last one, working as an assistant to a bail bondsman, led me to skip tracing, which seemed to suit my personality—someone with a problem with authority who had a logical enough mind that he could figure out how to find people. I'm not saying I was great at it, but I was better at it than anything else I could think of. And it kept food on the table and I didn't have to answer to anyone but myself.

What more could I want out of a job? But this? I was way out of my depth. Still, I smelled a payday big enough to keep the wolf from my door for a long time, and maybe enough money that I could visit my son for a week or so—let him know he had a father.

My hands were filthy. The bathroom was small and it smelled of disinfectant. I hit the hot water tap, but there was nothing but the short hissing sound of escaping air, so I settled for washing my hands in cold water. There was no towel, so I wiped my hands on my trousers, flipped off the light, and started to leave. But before I could take more than a step or two into the room I was hit with a tremendous blow to the gut. I doubled over in pain. I gasped for air. I tried to straighten up, but before I could manage even that, I was hit again on the back of the neck and then, before I could raise my arm to defend myself, another blow struck me on the side of the head. There might have been more, but I couldn't remember. My knees buckled under me and before I even hit the ground everything went black. ⚡

# A Step in the
# RIGHT DIRECTION

W HEN I CAME TO, I WAS STARING UP at the bottom of a dirty sink and my head felt like a flamenco dancer had done a number on it. It was the first time in my life I'd ever been knocked cold and, amazingly, the only time I'd ever taken a punch in the line of duty—somehow, I'd always managed to move fast to avoid being hit. I sat up and gingerly explored the back of my head with my hand. My hair was wet and matted. Blood, I thought, but when I looked at my fingers I found it was just water, from the leaky sink.

After pushing myself up slowly, I felt for my wallet. It wasn't there. A wave of panic shot through me. My life was in that wallet. I looked around and there it was, lying on the floor on the other side of the sink. I reached for it and opened it up. The Janus woman's check was right where I'd put it but what little cash I'd had was gone.

I was pissed. I should have been more careful, but usually

I see my potential attackers coming at me head on or, like a couple of nights before, in the rearview mirror. In the future, if there was one, I'd have to be more careful.

I wobbled into the bedroom. Everything seemed to be in place. I started to wonder about what happened. Was it the guy who had been following me earlier? Was this just a way of warning me off the case? And if so, why? And how did someone know I was even on the case?

Once outside, I found a phone booth and dialed Janus's answering service. I bluffed my way through, making like I was Harry Janus asking for his messages. It worked. There were several dating from more than a week back, including half a dozen from his wife. Two others were from a woman identified only as Carole. Both were urgent, but neither left a return number, which meant that Janus knew it, which also might mean it was the same Carole on the return address I found at the Janus home. Two other messages were from someone named Horst. The return number was in Germany. The second message, logged in just two days before Janus was killed, was simply, "Will not be able to offer any further assistance." I wrote all this down in my notebook, thanked the answer lady, and hung up.

It was nearly five o'clock. Quitting time.

The streets were still wet from a brief shower. I hopped on the subway at 50th and Seventh and was standing on the corner of my office block fifteen minutes later. I was starting to feel good. I tried to figure out why. The possible answer frightened me. It was the case. I was actually feeling good about what I was doing. And, what's more, it looked as if it wouldn't be over as quickly as I'd first thought, which meant that I might actually be able to tuck away a nice piece of change by the time it was all over.

It looked to me now as if Sally Janus might have been right about the death of her husband. It wasn't a coincidence that I was being followed. And it wasn't a coincidence that someone cold-cocked me in that hotel room. All of which meant that Harry Janus's murder was not a random act and, since the police weren't interested in the case, it was going to be up to me to find out who killed him and why.

Maybe this private detecting wasn't so bad after all. **⚡**

# Trivial
# PURSUITS

THE CALL OF THE PARADISE was a lot stronger than the call of my office and so, once I emerged from the subway, that's the direction in which I headed. The sky had cleared and the sun had begun to take its daily dive behind New Jersey, reflecting light off empty, green-tinted wine bottles that lined the gutters. Once the stench of fresh dog crap, most of it deposited by the neighborhood German shepherds and Dobermans, returned to my nose, I knew I was home.

Across the street, blocking the entrance to my office building, were the ever-present old men, perched precariously on grocery crates and folding chairs set up comfortably against the building in order to watch passersby. They were drinking beer and cheap wine, telling oft-repeated tales and playing dominoes. And so, rather than make a pit stop at my office before stopping at the PB&G, I crossed the street to avoid having to fight my way through a chorus of Spanish taunts and *espiritismo* curses.

The Paradise was about as empty as it ever gets. Most of the regulars were home either making more babies or batting around wives or girl friends, the only real exercise many of them ever get. Manny was on his break and Luis, his kid brother who was out of the slammer for a change, was tending bar. Unlike his brother Manny, Luis was not the friendly type. He had a chip on his shoulder, and white was definitely not his favorite color.

I had a couple of drinks, but it wasn't much fun staring at Luis's sour kisser, and there was no one else around to shoot the breeze with, so I decided to ditch the Paradise and head back to my office, where I'd make up the day's expense account while my imagination was still fueled by a couple of stiff belts of Johnny Walker.

Upstairs, I got a little surprise: my office had been broken into. Break-ins are not unusual in my part of town—I'd need an adding machine to tote up how many times my lock had been picked, jammed or busted. But this was an especially clumsy job. The door was smashed in, wood splinters covered the linoleum, and my office, usually a mess, was in even worse shape: papers strewn on the floor, drawers pulled out and their contents spilled to the floor, and the Morris chair was ripped to shreds. I kept little of value around, but what little there was—an answering machine, an old electric typewriter, a small tape recorder—hadn't been taken, which led me to believe that this wasn't a real break-in in the normal sense, but another message in case I didn't get the first. I was pissed, but there was little I could do about it. It's not as though the cops were going to be much help. All they'd do is scribble in their notebooks, and help themselves to my small supply of sugar for their bodega brand coffee.

After cleaning up the place, I checked my answering machine and found an invitation from Sally Janus for dinner. I checked my blank calendar and was unsurprised to discover that I was free. And I was hungry. Being a victim twice in one day seemed to have that effect on me.

⚭

DINNER WAS SERVED BY CANDLELIGHT. First, we talked about the case. She wanted to know everything. I told her almost everything, holding back only a few details, namely, my mugging, mostly because I was embarrassed about it. It was only after dinner, over a brandy, that I mentioned I'd gotten cold-cocked. She looked concerned.

"It's not going to keep you from continuing your investigation, is it?"

"I have a very low threshold for pain."

"But you're going to keep going, aren't you?"

"I guess...."

She leaned forward and touched my shoulder. "Where does it hurt?"

I pointed to the back of my head and she leaned over and kissed it gently. I was surprised and I felt a little uncomfortable, yet at the same time I was getting aroused. I debated with myself for a moment or two about what direction I'd like to take this. I couldn't quite figure out what was going on—the woman, who'd just lost her husband, seemed to be making a play for me. Or was she? Maybe she was just trying to manipulate me into staying on the case, as if mere money wasn't enough. I was tempted to take her up on what seemed to be a very interesting perk, but for a change good sense prevailed and I backed off. The last thing I needed was a complication in my life. This was business, and I decided to keep it that way. She obviously sensed my hesitation and steered the conversation in another direction.

"What made you become a detective?" she asked. "I'm not a detective, and I don't pretend to be."

"Sure you are, you just give yourself another name."

"Over the years, I've given myself lots of names."

"So how did you get into the business?"

"I was drifting, out of work, out of ideas, and someone offered me a job that didn't seem too demanding and fulfilled certain criteria, so I took it. And it suited me. Finding people, finding things, bringing them back to their rightful owner. It makes me feel virtuous."

"Does that mean that you aren't really virtuous?"

"You'll find out, won't you?"

"You like what you do, don't you?"

"Parts of it. And parts of it I hate. Sometimes I don't like myself very much, but then there are times other people don't like me very much either."

"What are you parts you do like?"

"I like sticking my nose into other people's business. I like to know what makes them tick. I like to know why they do the things they do. I like to watch people when they're not looking, when they think they're alone. I like to read other people's mail. I like to listen in on their private conversations. Let's face it, I'm a born sneak."

"Maybe you like it so much because you're dissatisfied with your own life?"

"That sounds suspiciously like psycho-babble to me."

"They say people often choose their profession because it fulfills some need in their own life."

"So you think I'm really trying to find myself ?"

"You think that's so off the wall?"

"Well, it's a little late to be thinking about that. I've made my choice and I'll live with it. The way I see it, you take a certain path in life and if you stay on it long enough you might as well go all the way and see where it leads."

"I don't know why you waste your time working up there in that slum. You seem like an educated man to me."

"Yeah, well, I don't know what that means, but thanks. Anyway, it's not as bad up there as you think. Everything's out in the open. Up there is what life's really like. It's ugly, but they don't try to hide it. What you've got down here, what your husband had, it's ugly, too. Only difference is down here you try to mask things by putting up lace curtains."

"Cynical, aren't we?"

"I suppose it goes with being nosy."

She was quiet for a minute, staring out into space. Finally, she said, "What do you think about Harry's death? You don't think it was a pimp, do you?"

"It's looking less likely."

"Do you think that beating you took and the break-in at your office had something to do with this?"

"Seems reasonable. Let me ask you something."

"Okay."

"You and your husband, were you getting along okay?"

"Don't tell me you suspect me?"

"Should I?"

Her body turned rigid. "Why the hell would I hire you to find out who killed him if I had anything to do with it?"

"That's a good question."

"And the answer?"

"It doesn't make sense that you would."

Her body loosened, though only slightly. "That's right. It doesn't. Why would you ask a question like that?"

"Because in order to track down whoever did it I have to know as much about your husband as possible."

"Look, I don't feel I have to apologize for the kind of relationship we had. We were consenting adults."

"I ought to talk to some people who knew him. Can you give me a list of names and numbers?"

"Yes, but I don't think it's going to do any good. They're all people I know and they would have told me anything that might have shed light on this thing."

"'Thing?'"

"You know what I mean."

"Tell me a story about Harry."

"What do you mean?"

"I mean, tell me the first thing about him that comes into your head."

"Well, this is going to sound stupid, but one day I was very upset because I'd purchased a pair of jeans from this kind of schlocky clothing store on Second Avenue. They were defective and when I took them back they refused to give me anything but store credit. I don't know why I was upset—it wasn't about the money. I kind of lost my temper with the clerk, which didn't do any good, of course. Later, when I told Harry about it and he saw how upset I was, he took me back to the store and confronted the clerk. He didn't lose his temper. He just reasoned with the man. And then when he couldn't get anywhere, he reasoned with the store manager. Eventually, they returned the money. You know, it wasn't about the money—it was that Harry took my side. He didn't say, 'Oh, let's just forget it. It was only a few dollars.' He had this enormous sense of fair play and justice." Her eyes started to well up. "And nothing seemed to fluster him. I never saw him lose his temper. Never."

She sighed and bit at her fingernail. "Listen, Swann, I want you to go to California and find out about that woman. I want to know who she is and what she had to do with my husband. I think that's where you might get an answer to this thing. You'll do that, won't you?"

"Maybe you won't like the answers I come back with."

"Maybe I won't, but I still want you to get them. I need to know who killed Harry and why. And I need to know more about him...things I should have known while he was alive. Will you go?"

"As long as you're paying the bills, lady, I'll go to the ends of the earth."

"Well," she said, "I hope you won't have to go quite that far." ⚐

# The Wings
## OF MAN

I WAS THE AMERICAN DREAM INCARNATE. One minute I was practically picking lice out of my hair and roaches out of my food, and the next I was getting ready to wing off to L.A. I didn't know whether Janus was aced out the way the cops thought or the way his wife thought, but it didn't really matter. I was on the payroll and if the boss wanted me to go to L.A., who was I to argue?

But first, in the little time I had left, I made a few phone calls to the late Harry Janus's New York friends. Sally Janus had been right. They didn't have much to say. None knew anything about his background; none had ever heard of Carole Cheney; all of them had only good things to say about him. He was generous. He was sensitive. He was kind. He was brilliant—to the point where if any of them needed information about anything, he was the one they would go to. "Had a mind like a steel trap," one of them told me. Another one marveled at his memory. "The guy never forgot a thing," he said. "He always used to joke that if I didn't want him to remember something I told him that I shouldn't tell him. And he was right. It was like he had a computer inside that head of his and he could access information faster than anyone I ever knew."

"He was always putting people together," one of his racquetball buddies told me. "He was very generous with his contacts. Never asked for a finder's fee. I used to joke that he was the 'ultimate contact.' You know that six degrees of separation thing? Well, it seemed like Harry was only one or two degrees away from anybody."

You would think maybe one of these friends might have some kind of theory as to why Harry Janus might have been down in Times Square on that particular night, some inkling of a dark side, but no. From what his friends thought of him, the only thing I could surmise was that he was down there planning to open a mission, trying to reclaim the souls of a few sinners, or handing out condoms.

I checked my bag—after informing security that I had packed a pistol, for which I showed them my permit. With time to kill before my flight took off, I bought the *Times*. I sat down in the waiting area and read all about the crises in various parts of the world and then, when I couldn't read anymore, I worked the crossword puzzle. I've had plenty of practice. There isn't much else to do on stakeouts and business hasn't been all that good lately. I'm hip to almost all the obscure words. Nigerian tribes, exotic winds, foreign capitals, early slaves, oriental nurses, eastern princes and princesses, harem rooms, Shakespearean characters—much of which is the result of having too much time on my hands to read. Besides, I like puzzles. I like filling in those little boxes with letters until the entire square of boxes is filled. It gives me a sense of accomplishment and completion. And sometimes, when I'm near the end, with only a few empty spaces left, and I can't come up with the answers, I'll just fill in a bunch of letters. Just to make the puzzle work.

The airplane cabin was hot, like El Barrio on a July day. I took off my jacket and put it on my lap. I fastened the seat belt and settled in for the five-hour-plus, coast-to-coast flight. I was a little nervous. I didn't like flying. I suppose it's a control thing. At least that's what the shrinks would probably say. Anyway, I was trying to think about other things when suddenly I felt the vibrations of the powerful engine and a sharp jolt as the sleek 747 jumbo jet began lumbering down the runway. Slowly at first, then picking up steam, the aircraft, gaining surprising grace as it accelerated, bumped once, twice, then finally lifted itself from the ground and was airborne. I looked out the window and could see the plane opening its angle to the earth and soon the aircraft, its nose pointed toward the heavens, its tail dipping earthward, penetrated the cloud cover. We banked left, leveled off, and headed west, away from the city. ⨍

# PART ❷

# LOS ANGELES
*New York to Los Angeles*

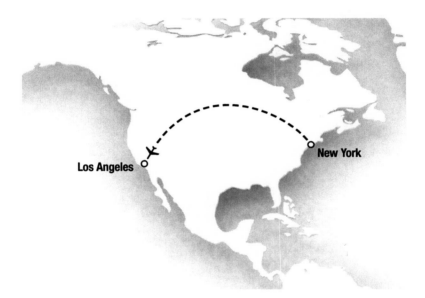

# California
## DREAMIN'

ITRIED NODDING OFF, but my mind was racing too fast and I couldn't sleep. Halfway into the trip I gazed down onto what I thought might be Missouri, where my son lived. Suddenly, I felt very lonely. I fixed that by having a drink and promising myself I'd stop off and see him on my way back. A convenient lie I knew I wouldn't make good on. So I had another drink.

Even though I'd logged more than five hours in the air by the time I got off the plane at LAX, it was still only two hours later than when I'd left New York. The miracle of modern technology. Five steps forward and three back. No friendly waves, familiar handshakes, back slaps, or loving kisses greeted me at the airport, since I knew no one in L.A., or the whole of California, for that matter.

L.A. was a new one on me. Sure, I'd read about it and sat through plenty of movies and TV shows, but that was only two-dimensional familiarity. You don't really get to know a place until you've set foot there, touched the ground, tasted the air, and drank in the character of the town. But I wasn't so sure that the character of this town, not to mention the air, was something I was going to be fond of.

After picking up my bag from the carousel, I was approached by one of those scary Hare Krishna kids who haunt the airports when they should be in school. She couldn't have been much more than 16. She wore that assembly-line, sweet, painted-on smile that's part of their uniform. She asked me if I'd seen the Divine Light. I told her I had: every night after I've had a few shots of Johnny Walker. That was not what she wanted to hear. I must have had the look of a sinner worth saving, because she stuck with me as I made my way through the airport, looking for a place to rent wheels. "Brother," she said, clutching a bunch of pamphlets against her chest. "Why don't you come and have dinner with us tonight? We will show you the true way."

"Honey," I said, "I've been following the true way my whole life and look where it got me."

"You mustn't give up hope, brother," she said plaintively. I eyed the white carnation behind her ear. It was starting to wilt. I began to feel sorry for her and all those like her. She'd been brainwashed into believing her life wasn't worth a plug nickel unless she could convince heathens like me that we were on the wrong spiritual path, on the precipice of disaster, and that the only true path to inner happiness and fulfillment was through her particular brand of religion.

"Abandon hope, ye who enter here," I announced cynically.

She looked at me quizzically. "There is always hope, brother," she said earnestly in a half-whine as she tugged at my sleeve like a lost puppy dog. This kid wasn't much different from the 13-year olds who come to New York and wind up on the Minnesota Strip selling their twats for some jive-ass pimp. But instead of selling sex, this kid was selling souls.

"Come home with us and you shall learn the law according to the Divine Light," she said. I was looking at her, but all I could see was this poor kid getting off the bus, train or plane and being pitched the same bullshit she was pitching me. I could see the enormous appeal in this approach. Catch some kid when he or she is only half awake, on the rebound from a home where no one gives a damn, and that was all she wrote. I thought about my kid and pangs of guilt shot through my belly.

"Kid," I said, "someday you'll learn what's really happening out here in the real world. Someday you'll wake up and find out that the Inferno was peanuts compared to what you go through in life. But take it from me, the answer isn't bailing out, covering your face with that sickly sweet smile and babbling about the Divine Light. Baptism by fire, kid, that's where it's at. The only way you can make it through life in one piece is by standing tough. Not by chanting mantras and shaving your head and accosting innocent travelers in airports."

She looked at me and shook her head. She'd finally had enough of me and took off to hit a more susceptible traveler, and I, having performed my social work for the day, pulled up in front of a rent-a-car booth.

Flashing a return smile at the Avis girl, I knew I could have gotten far more than just a car and map of the city, but that's all I was in the market for. The Kate Hudson type, she was probably biding her time between acting lessons in the A.M.s and P.M.s, hanging out at Spago until the movies snatched her up to play Kate Hudson parts. Next time I saw her it might be up there on the screen right alongside a Tom Cruise type.

Once I successfully negotiated for the car rental, I began to drive aimlessly around the city. Ostensibly, I was looking for a hotel nearest Chandler Boulevard, wherever the hell that was, but L.A. lends itself to aimless driving. In California, the automobile is God. They wax it, shine it, wash it, eat in it, sleep in it, screw in it, listen to church sermons in it, and worship it. Someone once wrote that in life there are three solitary pleasures: reading, masturbation and driving an automobile. I think maybe in L.A. you can scratch the first two. Thank God

I didn't have to repo cars out here. It might be worth my life.

It didn't take long to figure out that the sense of time in L.A. was all whacked out. Time zones change when you swap coasts, and so do concepts of time and distance. Places weren't measured in miles, but rather by the time it took to get there by wheels. Pile into the old heap, ooze onto the freeway, and a twenty minute drive is close. An hour? Not bad. Time is relative. Distance means nothing. It was the true Einsteinian universe. Everything moved all the time. Here, the world was connected by the automobile and sets of complex, intertwining freeways that stretched from Hollywood like giant tentacles penetrating through the hills and into the valley.

I was driving around getting a feel for the terrain, and before I knew it the sun was rising over the mountains. I pulled up in front of the Sheraton Hotel, just a stone's throw from Universal City where, for a couple of bucks, you could see how dreams were made and then maybe cop a few for yourself.

I got a room on what would have been the thirteenth floor if they'd had one. I slipped the bellhop a buck and then stepped out onto the terrace to check out the view. In front of me lay the valley; behind me, the Hollywood Hills. I stepped back inside, ordered breakfast from room service and then, after I'd eaten, I tried to get some sleep. But I was too excited, so I decided to bop on down to the pool for an hour or so just to get some color on those pale New York cheeks of mine. I had been in California a mere twelve hours and already I was under its spell. Though I had a twinge of guilt for relaxing on someone else's dime, I had to unwind and the hotel pool with its soothing sounds of splashing water and ice tinkling in hi-ball glasses seemed like the best place to do it.

I stepped out onto the terrace. It was unbearably hot and smoggy. I preferred the inside of my room where the temperature was a thermostatically controlled 64 degrees, about 20 degrees lower than outside. Outside, L.A. was sizzling, but inside it was New York cool. Funny, but whenever you strive for perfection you generally wind up in your not-so-distant past.

If I was going to make the poolside scene, I needed a bathing suit, so I made a quick trip to the hotel boutique, where I charged my purchase to my client. Then back upstairs, on with the suit, and fifteen minutes later I was stretched out on a lounge chair, strategically wedged between two shapely young female bodies, already greased and well-tanned, reflecting the smoggy California sunshine off the bared portions of their anatomy. I took off my shirt, adjusted my seat upward so I could catch all the action, then leaned back to enjoy myself.

"Isn't that Jay Leno?" the greased blonde, no more than twenty, her surfer's bleached hair tied severely behind her head, squealed to her pal, a brunette, similarly shaped and greased, lying next to her.

"Yeah, I think so. Isn't he cute? I'd give anything to meet him."

I thought of that kid back at the airport and tried to make a mental picture of her sitting there talking about star fucking. Jesus, the world was screwed up. My eyes flicked back and forth like a rattlesnake in heat. My neck began to ache from craning. But who cared? L.A. was great! What sights! What sounds! And I'd only seen the airport and the hotel. I blessed Harry Janus. I blessed Sally Janus for walking her dainty, well-manicured fingers through the Yellow Pages. I blessed everyone I could think of and then I dove into the tepid, chlorinated pool, swam a few laps.

Noon arrived much too quickly. A man has to have some sense of responsibility, doesn't he? Mine was purchased for a mere $350 a day. But in truth, I was anxious to meet this Cheney woman and solve the case. I wanted to fill in all those little, empty boxes.

On the way upstairs I picked up the L.A. *Times*. "Slasher Butchers 12th Victim." Another skid-row bum had bitten the dust. So it was an even dozen now. Crime took different forms out here in Lotus Land, I thought. Everything was on a larger, grander scale. Out here, everything was movie screen size. Back east, like with Harry Janus, you just got your ass shot off, or stabbed maybe in a fit of anger or because of the absence of another, more efficient weapon. But out in L.A., where there was always an eye out for a possible movie tie-in, it was your throat you had to watch. And damned if it didn't become a kind of contest. Almost like some sick   game show. Every murderer seemed to kill with an eye peeled for the previous record. Multiple murders were in. And the papers came up with some terrific, eye-catching names for their killers. The Slasher. The Zodiac Killer. The Black Dahlia Murderer. "Slasher Carves Up Another." "Slasher Slices His Way to Fame and Fortune." "Slasher's Scalpel Slits Tenth." Will he break Juan Corona's record? Two more and we can make a mini-series out of it.

I tossed the paper in the trash and jumped into the shower. I'd gotten sunburned. My body tingled, stung, then turned sensitive, as I dried myself carefully with a towel. I needed a shave, but the idea of running a razor across my face gave me the shivers.

Twenty minutes later, following hazy instructions from the concierge, I was off in my little red Honda pointed toward North Hollywood. I reached Chandler Boulevard and zeroed in on the Cheney residence. I parked across the street, knocked on the door of the large white and brown stucco hacienda-style house and waited. Inside, a dog barked. I knocked again and the dog barked louder. I was beginning to think no one was home. I was wrong.

"Quiet! Brutus! Quiet! Hold on, I'll be right with you," a voice called from inside the house. Brutus sounded hungry. I stepped back from the door and looked around. Nice place. A million and a half at least, I figured and that was probably on the low side, given what real estate was like. The dog kept barking. Maybe they ought to feed it every once in a while. There was a Mercedes in the driveway. Probably another in the garage. There were so many of those babies out here that they started looking like Ford Pintos. I wondered if there was much repoing work, just in case I decided to make a move.

The screen door swung open. I could see only a hand holding it ajar. Inside, it was dark. A woman's voice asked, "What do you want?"

"I'm looking for Carole Cheney," I said, trying to position myself in the way of the door so she couldn't close it on me.

"There is no Carole Cheney anymore, hon," she said in a lilting voice.

"Dead?"

"Nope."

"What then?"

"Remarried, hon."

She stuck her hand through the crack in the door and waved it at me so that I couldn't possibly miss the rock on her finger.

"You her?"

"That's right. What can I do for you?" She opened the door so I could get a better look at her. She was wearing an unbuttoned man's shirt over a bikini and had flaming red hair. She looked familiar to me, but I couldn't quite place her. But then maybe it was because attractive women like her were a dime a dozen in L.A. and chances are she got her hair color out of the same bottle half the women at the hotel I was staying at did.

"I'd like to talk to you a couple of minutes. Can I come in?"

"Not until I know who you are and what you want."

"My name's Henry Swann and I'm a private investigator."

"Oh yeah? So what do you want with me?"

"I'm looking for someone...."

"And?" she said, smiling.

"I think maybe you knew him."

"You got ID?"

I showed her my driver's license.

"Don't you have anything like a badge or an ID?"

"That's only in the movies," I lied. The truth was, I didn't have a private investigator's license, so I was no more official than the kid who parked cars at the hotel.

"Okay, well, the place is a mess. Come on round back by the pool. We can talk there."

The door slammed shut, and I figured I was supposed to find my way back there. I walked around the house, passing precisely manicured lawns and shrubbery that looked as if they had been painted green. The grounds, in fact, looked like they had come straight from the prop department of a movie studio.

The ex-Mrs. Cheney, who had a terrific body, was stretched out on a lounge chair beside the kidney-shaped pool by the time I made it out to the back. She was lying on her stomach with her bikini top unstrapped. By her head was a wrought iron glass-topped table. On it, a half filled glass, a radio tuned to a rock station, and a pair of oversized sunglasses.

"Sit down, honey," she said. "Take a load off. Got a bathing suit underneath all that?"

"Nope."

"Too bad. Hot as hell, isn't it? Been out in the sun, huh?" she said, noticing my burn. "*Tourista*, right? You'll feel it later. Listen, do me a favor, huh? Let me know when ten minutes are up, okay? I don't want to get too much sun on my back. I'm fair skinned, you know. I burn easily."

"My pleasure," I said. "Name Harry Janus mean anything to you?" I asked.

"Can't say that it does."

"You're sure?"

"I'm sure, sweetie. I'm very sure. How's about a drink? You look thirsty."

"Not a bad idea," I said. "It's hot."

"'We're havin' a heat wave,'" she sang. "'A tropical heat wave.' Help yourself. Over there." She pointed to a bar at the other end of the pool. "Gin and tonic. Make it long and tall, which is how I like my men." She winked.

I made her a gin and tonic, myself a scotch.

"Thanks, sweetie," she said, taking the drink from me. "Listen, why don't you take off that jacket and relax. This is L.A., honey. No one wears a jacket around here except for the help."

I took off my jacket, draped it on the back of my chair, and pulled out the photo of Harry Janus. "Recognize this man?"

"Hand me my shades, honey." I did. She squinted through them at the photo. A moment passed, then she handed it back to me along with her sunglasses.

"Well?"

"Ought to. He's my ex. Calling himself Harry what now?"

"Janus."

"Well, what do you know, what d'ya say? He was Jason Cheney when I knew him."

"And when was that?"

"Jesus, seems like a lifetime now, but I guess it must have been maybe fifteen years ago. You know, out here you tend to lose track of time. It all sorta runs together. No seasons out here, sweetie. Every day seems like the next. It was back in the early '80s. That's when we broke up. Haven't seen him since. Hey, my ten up yet?"

"A couple more. Tell me about him."

"Why?"

"Because he's dead and because I've been hired to find out who killed him and why."

"Dead, huh? That's tough. Real tough." She was silent a moment. I tried to get a good look at her to see how she was taking it, but she was lying on her cheek, her face distorted by the chair cushion, and the sun was glaring in my eyes.

"So you're a private dick?"

"Uh, yeah. That's right."

She lifted her face and smiled. "Just like Mike Hammer and Philip Marlowe. Now, this is getting interesting," she said, rubbing her hands together with glee. She was taking this pretty well, I thought. And she was a damn good liar, too. I would've bet Harry Janus's socks that she'd seen him when he was in L.A. a few weeks earlier. But I didn't think there was any need to call her on that now. I'd just string her along for a while and see what developed.

"How long were you two lovebirds married?"

"Let's see now. Maybe three years. But who was counting? Hey, how's about a refill?"

"Why not?" I said. I took her glass and mine and made the trip over to the bar and back. I set her drink down on the table and caught an eyeful of the bulge her breasts made against the lounge chair. I matched that with my own bulge in my pants. "Thanks, hon," she said, taking another sip from her glass.

"Your ten minutes are up," I said.

"Thanks, sweetie. Hey, wanna do me a favor and hook this up for me, *por favor*. It's kinda hard to reach."

I touched her back and my hand lingered. It was hot from the sun. I fumbled with the strap and it took me a couple seconds but I finally managed to hook it up. I felt like a kid trying to get to second base. She smiled. Believe me, it was a very friendly smile. She flipped over and sat up. "I met him while he was appearing at some little club on the Strip. We got hitched a few months later. That's all there is."

"What do you mean, appearing?"

"With his group, hon."

"What group?"

"You must be kidding?"

"No. What group?"

"You didn't know? You never heard of him?"

"No."

"He was Jason, of Jason and the Argonauts. You must've heard of them."

"Can't say I have."

"Jesus, I thought everyone had. They were *tres* big back in the late '70s. 'Stomp Out the Fires of My Heart' was their big one. It was on the charts for something like a month or two.

Sold somewhere over a million. I've got the platinum record to prove it. Listen, come on inside and I'll show you some pictures of Jason when he was on top," she said, rising from her chair. She slipped into her wedgies and adjusted her tits.

"I thought the place was a mess," I said.

She grinned. "Not the bedroom, hon." 𝆏

# Those Oldies
# BUT GOODIES

**"T**IME'S UP, SWEETIE".

"Huh?" I grunted groggily, zonked half out of my mind from the combination of alcohol, the heat, lack of sleep and the physical exertion. I lay there sweating like Nixon during the presidential debates, spread eagle on my stomach in the middle of the king-sized bed, while the Cheney woman wiggled sexily back into her bikini.

"Time to get up, hon. The old man'll be back any second and it wouldn't be too cool if he caught us up here in what the *Enquirer* might call 'a compromising position.' In flagrante, you know. So throw your clothes on and we'll go back downstairs and, uh, finish our business."

I got up, found my pants where I'd dropped them on the floor and pulled them on. "Keep the shirt off, lover, in case you want to get some more California sunshine on that hairy he-man's chest of yours. Mmmmm, I just go out of my mind for hairy chests."

"My father was a gorilla and my mother was the bearded lady in the circus," I cracked, while my arm, which no longer seemed to be controlled by my brain, tried to find its way into my shirt sleeve. "I think I've had enough sun for today. Your husband always home this early?"

"He's the boss, hon. He owns the store, so he comes and goes as he pleases."

"What's he do?"

She laughed. "The silver screen, lover, what else? He's a big-time movie mogul, like half this town. And the other half is trying to get in to see him and his mogul amigos."

"That so," I said, as I followed the ex-Mrs. Cheney's undulating backside down the stairs.

Walking through the living room I saw what must have been Jason Cheney's platinum record staring down at me from its place above the fireplace. The smog had burned off and the brilliant California sunlight, filtered through the bay window and reflected off the platinum ridges, blinded me momentarily.

Outside, we settled down by the pool again. Carole lay on her back and I took a chair that faced away from the sun. "Aren't you worried about aging from the sun?" I asked, as I put on my sunglasses.

She smiled. "There's nothing that can't be fixed by modern science, baby. A nip and a tuck in the right place can do wonders. Do you think anyone actually looks the way they are out here?" She laughed. "Honey, if I had a buck for all the stitches on all the faces out here I would be a very rich woman. Rich enough so that I'd never look any different than the way I do now. Smoke?" she asked, pulling a cigarette case out from underneath her chair.

"Gave it up," I said.

She laughed, adjusted her bikini top, then opened the case and took out a joint. "No, lover, not that kind of smoke. I'm talking about primo stuff. Rocky Mountain high? You know, grass, reefer madness, a joint, Mary Jane, herb, marry-jew-wanna, whatever you call it back east. My hubby, Jackie-baby, scored some dynamite stuff the other day. Straight off the farm from 'south of the border, down Mexico way!'" she sang gaily.

"No thanks. I think I'll stick to whiskey. I've already got a good start on my liver, so I might as well finish the job."

"Suit yourself, sweetie," she said, lighting up and taking a long toke.

"Your husband deal on the side?"

"Jack?" she laughed. "No, sweetie, not Jack. He's a consumer, not a retailer. He's got this connection who sells him stuff straight from the source. It's just for his own personal use...and a very select group of good friends, if you get my drift."

I wanted to get my business done and get the hell out of there before her husband showed up. I didn't think he'd appreciate his wife entertaining strange, hairy-chested men in the middle of the afternoon—especially the kind of entertaining we'd been doing.

"Did Cheney have any thing to do with drugs?"

"Jason? What do you think, hon? He was a musician, sweetie, and you know their reputation with mind altering substances." She laughed and rolled her eyes wildly. "I mean, he wasn't any dopehead, if that's what you're thinking, but he enjoyed a good high every so often. But who doesn't, right? With the kind of people he knew, he could get all he wanted just by snapping his fingers. So what would be the point? As far as I knew the only law Jason ever broke was buying and using the stuff, not selling it. That and maybe breaking the laws of nature every once in a while," she winked.

"Are you that sure about your husband?"

"Jack's a pussycat, lover. He wouldn't get mixed up in anything as sordid as that. He likes to keep his hands clean. He's got a reputation to protect. He wants to be the next Steven Spielberg. He wouldn't risk every thing by getting busted for drugs."

"But I bet he knows plenty of others into that scene, doesn't he?"

"Jack knows a lot of people, and some of them are into some pretty heavy stuff, if you know what I mean. Listen, there's mucho weirdo stuff going down in this town. Drugs are only the surface. There are all kinds of things being bought and sold."

"I'm only interested in Harry Janus or Jason Cheney or whoever the hell he was."

She shook her head and shrugged. "I'm afraid I can't help you there, sweetie."

I glanced at her watch lying on the glass table. It was getting late and her husband would be home soon. "I've got to be going..."

"What's the hurry, lover?" she said, fixing her sunglasses to shield her eyes. "Jack doesn't mind me having an occasional peccadillo. As a matter of fact, he kind of encourages it." She looked up at me, pushed her sunglasses further toward the tip of her nose, and smiled coyly. "You see, he's a regular B-movie queen, hon," she let her wrist go limp. "But it would've been *tres* bad manners if we'd stayed upstairs. So, how about another drink, lover?"

"No thanks. Why don't you tell me more about Janus."

"You mean Cheney, hon. I don't know anything about Janus." She leaned back, shifted her sunglasses to the top of her head and closed her eyes as she aimed her face to the sun. "Nothing to tell, lover. Most of the time we were married he was on the road. There was a big demand for Jason and the Argonauts, you know. Lots of screaming teeny-boppers and adoring fans. Disgusting, huh? Jason just ate it up. His group and his groupies probably knew him better than I ever did."

"So what was the attraction?"

She shrugged. "You get up there on stage with thousands of people hanging on your every word, your every move, it's an aphrodisiac. He represented possibilities for me and everybody else he came in contact with."

"What kind of possibilities?"

"You think I was born in a place like this? Uh-uh. I'm from

a little town in Wisconsin. I came here, like everyone else, to change my life...only I didn't have the talent. I knew that, and in order to make it I had to attach myself to someone who did. That's where Jason came in. But don't get me wrong. He treated me right, not like some of those other assholes around him. They liked to whack women around. Jason wouldn't have any of that. I once saw him get into it with one of his musicians after the dude smacked some chick. After he beat the crap out of him, he fired his sorry ass."

"Did you love him?"

"It was a chemical thing, lover. We just couldn't keep our hands off each other. For a while, at least. But lust cools and then reality sets in. But reality with Jason was okay, too. So long as I let him do his thing, it was cool."

"And what was his thing?"

"You know, I never even asked. Wasn't that terribly irresponsible of me?"

"What about his past?"

"What past are you referring to, lover?"

"Like where he came from?

"Someplace else. But everybody around here comes from someplace else."

"How did you meet?"

"Oh, gosh, how I do so love tripping down Memory Lane. How did we meet? Just like a fairy tale. It was at one of his concerts."

"You were a groupie?"

"Please, sweetie, you can't possibly think so little of me, even though we've just met. No, I was not a groupie. I went to the gig with friends and afterwards we went backstage and were introduced."

"And you fell immediately in love."

"Hey, who's telling this story anyway? No, we did not immediately fall in love, at least I didn't. He was real sexy but he wasn't exactly my type. Do you know what my type is?"

"Haven't a clue."

She winked. "Anyway, he called and asked me out the next day. I said okay. I didn't have anything better to do and he seemed exciting."

"Was he?"

"You bet. Everything he did had that little edge of danger. I'll tell you, after one date they really did have to stomp out the fires of my heart..."

"Why didn't you ask anything about his past?"

"Sweetie, why ruin a good thing? It made him that much more attractive. I mean, how many real mysteries are there in life? You know everything, there's nothing left to know. Know what I mean? Besides, part of what kept us together as long as we were was that I didn't know everything about him. He'd tell all kinds of stories about himself, but I knew most of them weren't true. It was as if he made himself up as he went along. He had this talent for telling you what you wanted to hear."

"So how come you're not still married to him?"

"Because he's dead. You said so yourself."

"I mean, before he died."

"Evolution."

"Evolution?"

"Sure. Everything evolves. Even the mystery couldn't keep us together forever. I grew. He grew. We all grew. Apart. But even after we split up I was still attracted to him. You know, it wasn't only that he had rhythm. He was smart, too. He wasn't one of those others, the kind who can't even tie their own shoes. Music was just his way of making a living, his way of expressing himself...at the time. A means to an end."

"What end?"

She shrugged. "Beats me. But he had one. I know that."

"How do you know?"

"Because that's the way he was, that's how. He used to say that, in the end, he'd just burn out and be a thin wisp of smoke, disappearing into thin air."

"Where can I find the members of his group?"

"Originally, there were six of them. You know those idiots actually used to dress up like Greek soldiers when they went on the road. The shorts, the armor plated helmets, the whole bit. Wild, huh? Hey, am I getting too red?"

"No, you're fine. Where are they now?"

"Where are they now?" she repeated. She counted them off on her fingers. "Frankie's dead. Killed in a car crash on the Ventura freeway one night. Jesus, what a crack-up that was. He was burned to a crisp, like a well-done burger at Jack in the Box. The other driver walked away without a scratch. Life is weird, ain't it? The only way they could identify him was through his teeth. Good thing he had'em, huh? Happened about a year after the group broke up."

"Why was that?"

"You mean the group breaking up?"

"Yeah."

"I don't know. I guess their time had come. Got a fag?"

I shook my head.

"Oh, yeah, I forgot, you don't smoke. Well, that's cool. I gave it up anyway."

"What about the others?"

"Others? Oh, yeah." She tapped the side of her head. "Y'know, the sun out here fries the brains. But you look so good with a tan, huh? Anyway, Bill killed himself. Jumped off the Golden Gate one night. Numero 500, I do believe. If he'd've lived they probably would've given him some kind of medal. If you ask me, he was probably flying high as a kite on something mind-altering. Zoom! Splat! The asshole couldn't even swim. Can you believe it? Al disappeared in the Bermuda Triangle. Buddy joined up with some biker group, the Straight Satans, I think. Last I heard he was one of the oldest bikers left in the state. I think he might be in Chino for dealing. I seem to remember hearing something like that. Far as I know Mike's still playing dates whenever and wherever he can."

"That's quite a graduating class. Where can I find Mike?"

"Try under a rock."

"Seriously."

"What makes you think I'm not serious? But you might try Jake's down on the Strip. He's been known to hang out there between gigs."

I was about to offer to rub suntan lotion on her back, purely as a means to obtain more information, you understand, when the sound of a powerful car engine filled the air. The dog began barking again. "It's the man of the house, Brutus," she shouted, as she jumped up. "Shut up! Daddy's home!"

"Time to hit the road," I said, getting to my feet.

"Don't be ridiculous, lover. Jack'd love to meet you. He's just crazy about all my friends."

The front door slammed shut and a moment later Jack Sharp, in his late 40s, medium height, receding hairline, slim, wearing faded blue jeans, blue blazer and Gucci loafers, sauntered into the back yard. Highball in hand, Jack, dragging a beach chair behind him, entered our tight little circle. I rose and offered my hand. "Henry Swann," I said.

"And this," the ex-Mrs. Cheney said, before her husband could answer for himself, "is my loving husband, Jack Sharp, or as he used to be known, Schwartz." Sharp flushed visibly and shook my hand.

"Business reasons," he explained sheepishly.

"Also hides the roots, doesn't it, dear?"

"We won't talk about roots, Carole, darling," he said. "That's some burn you got there, Mr. Swann," Sharp said. "Are you here on business or pleasure?"

"Business. I was just asking your wife here a few questions concerning her ex-husband, Jason Cheney."

"Where's Brutus, dear?" Sharp asked, turning to his wife.

"Locked in the garage, where he should be. He's a royal pain in the ass. That goddamn barking drives me up a wall."

"How the hell is he going to protect you if he's locked up

in the garage? I've asked you not to do that, Carole. It's not fair to the poor animal. He's got to be able to run around. He'll get neurotic otherwise."

"So he'll join the rest of us. I've got a doggie psychiatrist all lined up."

"He'll forget all his training."

"Well, let him run around when you're here. He gives me the creeps. I have the feeling he's going to attack me instead of some imaginary intruder. He's your dog, Jack. Why don't you take him to the studio with you?"

"That would defeat the whole purpose of having him, wouldn't it? He's here for your protection. Ever since that Simpson thing..."

"Isn't he sweet?" she said, turning to me. "He thinks now that O. J.'s back out on the street, he's going to terrorize all us white women. Well then, Jack, love of my life, how about a big, strong bodyguard. Like Mr. Swann here." She obviously enjoyed making trouble.

"What kind of questions, Mr. Swann?" Sharp asked, turning his attention back to me.

"Cheney's been murdered back in New York and I've been hired to find out who did it. I thought your wife might be able to help."

"And have you, dear?"

"I try my best, lover."

Sharp just smiled and looked back at me, as if for some help and understanding. "I don't really see how she could, Mr. Swann. She hasn't seen or heard from him in years. Their marriage was not the best, you know."

"Not at all like ours, huh, lover?"

I was beginning to pity poor Mr. Sharp. This woman could turn anyone queer. "Not a bit," he said, smiling, though it was a smile that looked like it had a lot of suppressed violence behind it. "Are you planning to stay in California long?" Sharp asked.

"Just as long as it takes."

"Well then, how about joining us for dinner. We've got a wonderful Mexican cook..."

"She's off," Carole said quickly. "But stay anyway. Jack's a load of laughs. He's one hell of a storyteller, right Jack? Keeps them rollin' in the aisles."

"Thanks, maybe another time," I said. I couldn't quite picture myself having a cozy little dinner with these two.

"Jack, baby, why don't you get into a suit and take a dip? It'll cool you off. You must be hotter 'n hell sitting there in your jeans."

"Good idea," he said. "I'll go upstairs and change. Nice meeting you, Mr. Swann. Perhaps we'll meet again."

Sharp rose and walked toward the house. I got up to leave.

"You don't have to go just yet, lover. Jack'll be upstairs for at least fifteen minutes. He always takes a shower before he goes in the pool. He's a real nut about cleanliness. Come on over here and cool off these hot lips of mine."

"I've got to be moving along," I said.

"Well, if you've got to go you've got to go. Where're you staying? In case I think of something important."

"Sheraton Universal."

"Well, you'll be hearing from me, lover. In fact, you might even be hearing from Jack. I think he took a liking to you."

"Lucky me," I said. "How long you two lovebirds been sharing the same nest?"

"Five wonderful, glorious, fun-filled years. Jack makes loads of money. He used to be in the record business, but now he's into film and he's very successful. *Mucho dinero*," she said, her face lighting up as she rubbed two fingers together. She got up from her chair. "I'll walk you up front."

At the front of the house we stopped and she moved closer to me. She rubbed her bare leg up against mine and a shiver went up my back. "Keep in touch, lover," she said, kissing me on the mouth, her hand squeezing at my crotch. It was a very nice way to say goodbye. I slipped a couple of fingers down the back of her bikini as our tongues met. What would the neighbors say, I wondered?

Our goodbyes completed, I jumped into my little red Honda and aimed it toward my hotel. As I pulled away I looked back over my shoulder. Carole Cheney was still standing on her front lawn. She waved and blew me a kiss. Out of the corner of my eye I was sure I saw someone watching me from the upstairs window of the Sharp house. The curtains ruffled and then there was no one.

"No need to get upset, Jackie baby," I muttered. "It was only our way of saying goodbye." ⚐

# The Mexican
# HAT DANCE

B ACK AT THE HOTEL, there was a message from Jack Sharp, suggesting we meet the next morning for breakfast. Maybe he thought I was screen material and was going to offer me a role in his next epic. Or maybe he was going to make like the outraged husband and give a go at punching me out. I was starting to regret my little tryst with his wife. Sometimes, when you're away from home, out of your element, you do crazy things, things you would never ordinarily do. That was one of them. The last thing I needed was one more enemy.

I went upstairs to take a nap. Three hours later I was showered, changed, and down in the hotel bar. Nursing a drink, I tried to put things together. In particular, I was trying to get a picture of Harry Janus. But it wasn't easy. I had this sneaking suspicion that I was dealing with a man who wasn't really ever there. Like he was a figment of someone's, everyone's imagination. In New York he was one thing, in L.A. another. And the profile

I was trying to put together of him didn't make sense. He was a man whose life left no fingerprints, a man of smoke. Even the photograph of him I carried around in my pocket did little good. His face was obscured by his beard and when I looked into his eyes, they were blank, as if there was nothing there behind them. Yet the longer I looked into them the more I was compelled to look deeper—looking for something I wasn't even sure was there.

I sat at the bar, absently packing away handfuls of peanuts and drinking cheap house scotch. At one point, I looked over my shoulder, out into the lobby, and thought I saw Jack Sharp. He was standing next to a pillar, talking to a small man who had his back to me. I debated with myself as to whether or not I should go out and say hello, but decided that the last person I wanted to talk to was Sharp. I nursed my drink, and when I turned around again, he, or the person I took to be him, was gone.

A half hour later, I hopped into my little red Honda and headed out toward Sunset Strip and Jake's to find Mike Pitts or any other Argonaut who might be in town. As I rode the Hollywood freeway, the sun played hide and seek behind the hills, but as soon as I hit Sunset Boulevard the sky seemed to darken all at once and suddenly day was night. I was lost. Finally, I pulled over to the side and checked my street map.

Twenty minutes later, I parked the car in the lot and went inside. A band, dressed in Hawaiian shirts and faded blue denim studded with sequins and silver, played country-western music. Skirting the dance floor, I took a seat at the bar and ordered a club soda. I paid the tab and asked about Pitts. The bartender, a nice looking, all-American type with flaxen hair the color of Michelle Pfeiffer's, wrinkled his forehead and tried looking pensive. "Pitts?" he said, running his hand through his thick, blond, surfer's hair. "Yeah, he comes in now and then. Haven't seen him for a while, though. Probably picked up a gig somewhere."

"Wouldn't happen to know where he lives, would you?"

He laughed. "Even he don't know where he's going to live from one day to the next."

"Yeah, well, that's the way it is sometimes. Know anyone who might know where he's working now, or maybe where he's staying?"

He thought for a moment. I knew he was thinking because he was scratching his head. The Stanislavski method, I believe. "Yeah, I guess Sweet Lou might know. He's the dude over there at the corner table with the two babes hanging all over him." I glanced over in the general direction. Sweet Lou was hard to miss. I paid for my drinks, tipped the bartender, though not nearly as well as I would have Manny, then picked my way through a dozen or so undulating bodies on the dance floor.

Sweet Lou, double-teamed by a pair of two sharp looking numbers in low-cut tops and short skirts, looked to be about forty. He was fat, dressed in a purple tuxedo jacket and frilly pink shirt, and his arms were draped around the girls' shoulders.

"You Lou?" I inquired poetically.

A cigarette dangling carelessly from the corner of his mouth, Bogie style, he looked up sleepily. "You talkin' to me?"

"Anyone else here named Lou?"

"So what do you want?" he sighed.

"Sorry to wake you." I pulled up a chair and sat down. He had a drink in front of him, along with a half-empty box of chocolates. It was easy to see where he got his name. He popped a chocolate in his mouth and asked, "Want one?" pushing the box toward me. "Chocolate covered cherries. Imported. Best money can buy. Better than Godiva. Better than Kron. Twenty-eight bucks a pound. Criminal, ain't it?"

"Yeah, maybe someone ought to dial 911."

"Maybe this is more your speed." He pulled a box out from under his chair and offered it to me. "Liqueur filled. Smuggled in from Switzerland. Shit, you'd think they'd have better things to do than hound people over a box of chocolates."

"I'll pass," I said.

"You ain't diabetic or something, are you?" he asked, licking his pudgy little fingers one at a time.

"No, but it's prom time and I've got to watch my complexion."

The girls laughed. Sweet Lou was much too busy sampling chocolates to bother. "Yeah, man, I can dig it," he said, after he'd downed another chocolate-covered cherry and was greedily eyeing the other box.

"Listen," I said, "I hate to break up this lovely party, but I'm looking for Mike Pitts and I was told you might be able to help me find him."

"Who told you that?"

"Does it matter?"

"Nope." He popped chocolate-covered cherries into the mouths of his two lady friends, then helped himself to another. "You've got employment for him, perhaps?"

"Could be."

He grinned. "That's bullshit, man. What are you, the heat?" he said, rearranging the box of chocolates so that the empty wrappers were lined up at one end.

"No."

"Then why you looking for him? I can't think of any reason why anyone would be looking for that loser, except maybe he owed them money."

"I'm a writer. I'm doing a story on old rock and roll groups and I want to interview Pitts. There may be some cash in it for him."

"And me?"

"Public service doesn't do it for you, huh?"

He shook his head.

"How about love for your fellow man?"

He shook his head again.

"Well then, if you play your cards right, maybe the Good Fairy will leave a box of Jujubes under your pillow."

He laughed. So did the girls. Then, I guess, to celebrate laughter, he fed all three another chocolate-covered cherry. The box was empty now.

"He's working a gig down in the Marina. At least that's the last I heard. Some singles joint called 'Mount Olympus.'"

"Thanks," I said, laying a ten spot on the table. "Buy yourself and the girls a box of M&M's on me."

"Thanks, man," Sweet Lou said, pocketing the dough.

"Melt in your mouth, not in your hands."

Weaving my way in and out of unfamiliar streets, I finally found the sleazy-looking singles joint nestled amongst newer and classier lounges in Marina del Rey. Inside, there was a long bar and several small tables surrounding a dance floor. It was too early for the place to be jumping, so the band was playing listlessly to no more than half a dozen customers. The dance floor was empty. A television set, tuned to the Dodger game, hung over the bar. I sat down and ordered another club soda.

"Which one is Pitts?" I asked the bartender.

"The drummer," he said glumly, wiping nonexistent rings from the bar.

"Do they have a break soon?"

"I guess."

I nursed my drink and watched the Dodger game until the middle of the third inning, when the band stopped playing. I left my drink on the bar and walked toward the stage. As Pitts was about to disappear into the backroom, I tapped him on the shoulder. "You Mike Pitts?"

He turned and looked me over. "Maybe. Who's askin'?"

"Got something to hide?"

"What do you want?" He was a scrawny-looking specimen who looked like he'd just crawled out from inside a bottle of Dexedrine. He had deep-set eyes, a crooked nose and ears that stuck out from left field. His skin looked like someone had taken sandpaper to it. He spoke with a slight speech impediment that made it difficult to understand what he was saying.

"How about I buy you a drink?"

"What for?"

"For old times' sake."

"I don't even know you."

"You will, and I'm sure you'll remember me fondly. What're you drinking?" He fell into deep thought for a moment, either thinking what he wanted or whether he should talk to me. When he asked for a margarita the dilemma was solved. I returned to the bar, picked up my own drink and grabbed one for Pitts. We took a table near the back. Pitts, a nervous fellow whose fingers were continually tap dancing on the table, his drink, or anything else within striking distance, took a swallow and said, "So what's the story?"

"I want to know about Jason Cheney."

Pitts got nervous. His body tensed. His fingers speeded up. Rat-a-tat-tat, like a machine gun on amphetamines. "Christ, I ain't seen him for ten, fifteen years. He just disappeared, man. Poof! Like he was never even here. What do you want to know about him for?" he asked suspiciously, methodically licking salt from the rim of the glass.

"I'm doing one of those 'where are they now' stories and I want to find out what happened to him after he left the Argonauts."

"I don't hardly know where the hell I am now," he cackled.

"Look, pal, there might be a lot more in this for you than just a couple margaritas. Why don't you just think a little harder."

"I just got through tellin' ya, I don't know nothing more about the man. What's over is over. Y'understand?"

I peeled off a twenty and laid it on the table. Silence. I peeled off another. I didn't know how much further I was willing to go, but I didn't have to wonder because at that point Pitts looked around nervously, then snatched the two bills off the table and stuffed them into his shirt pocket. "Last I heard, man, and that was well over ten years ago, he was down in Mexico. He was into, whaddya call it, man? You know, they study man and bones and shit like that."

"Anthropology? Archaeology?"

"Yeah, that's it, man. Shit, he was always running off his mouth about the history of man. Very heavy stuff, y'know? I mean way back. Not just a couple hundred years. He was on a kick about some Chinaman bones. I forget what they were called, man. I keep thinking food. Duck, maybe."

"Peking?"

"Yeah, that's it, man. Peking Man. He said it would be worth a fortune to find them bones. Not to mention all the newsprint the dude who found them would get. He'd be talking about that and then, the next minute, he'd be off on some tangent about the Aztecs, the Incas, the pyramids, shit like that. Man, he was one crazy dude. Smart, but crazy."

"And the last time you heard from him he was down in Mexico?"

"Yeah, Acapulco, but like I said, man, that was years ago. It was just after the group broke up. He called me once. He was all excited, you know? He talked about getting involved in something real big that was going to change his life. Said something about this cat he was staying with—"

"Who was that?"

"You got me, man."

"Think."

"His name...Jesus, man, it was a long time ago." Pitts looked longingly into my eyes. I got the message, reached into my wallet and put another ten on the table. "I'm thinking maybe his name was..." He smacked his head a couple of times. "Some funny sounding Indian name. Sitting Bull."

"I don't think so."

"Something like a bird." "Hawk?"

"Nah."

"Eagle?"

"Yeah, that's it. Eagle Eyes, something like that. He said I wouldn't hear from him for a while. He was dead right about that. Ain't heard from him since. That's all I know. Look," he said, glancing at his watch, "I gotta split."

"Wait a second," I said, grabbing his arm. "Where did Cheney come from? Where did he grow up?"

"If he ever said, I sure as hell don't remember. He never mentioned no family. Ask his wife. You met her? She's a real pisser, man."

"We've met."

"Yeah, well, if she don't know I sure don't. I was just an employee, man. Just one of five."

Again Pitts tried to leave, but I held onto his arm. "Know where I can find Buddy Phillips?"

"He was in the can, but he ain't no more."

"Where then?"

Pitts laughed. "Try Boot Hill. Got his throat cut up there in Chino couple weeks ago. Probably had something to do with dealing. Dude never was known for his smarts. Even back when we were in the group, he always had one scam or another going."

"Did he deal on the outside?" I asked, sniffing a possible connection between him and Sharp.

"Does a bear shit in the woods, man? Anything to make a buck. That's what got him in the slammer in the first place. He was busted with maybe fifty pounds of grass, some H, and a whole shitload of E. He cried frame all the way to the can."

"Where'd he get it?"

"Are you, crazy, man? Even if I knew, you think I'd be telling you?" He laughed nervously. "You could be heat."

"Do I look like a cop?"

"Man, nowadays nobody looks like what they're supposed to. You don't think I buy this crap about being a writer, do you?"

"Where'd the drugs come from?"

"What do you mean, where'd they come from?"

"What part of the world?"

He fiddled with his glass. He was thinking. I could practically see those little gray cells working overtime. Finally, he said, "I don't know. Mexico? Is that it?"

"Did Cheney have anything to do with drugs?"

"He wasn't no cokehead, if that's what you mean."

"Did he deal?"

"No way. He was too busy with his music and that goddamn archaeology crap."

"Name Jack Sharp mean anything to you?"

Pitts did a little jig in his seat but remained silent. It was okay. I had his answer.

"What do you know about him?"

"Hey, what is this? Twenty questions?"

I stared him down.

"He was in the music business. Name was Schwartz back then. Changed it after he got into flicks. I did a little business with him. He got some bookings for me."

"Then he knew Cheney."

"Maybe. But he couldn't've known him well. Jason didn't get himself involved in the business end of things. Frankie took care of most of that. Jason liked to think of himself as an artiste," Pitts said sarcastically, drawing out the last syllable and flashing a wry smile. I got the distinct feeling the group wasn't always one big happy family.

"Does Sharp have anything to do with the drug trade now?"

"How'm I supposed to know? Anyway, you came here to talk about Cheney, not drugs, not Sharp. It's gettin' late. I gotta split."

The last of the Argonauts, an endangered species, disappeared into a backroom. I had turned to leave when Pitts popped his head back out.

"Hey, man," he called. "One more thing. I want you to know that it was Frankie and me wrote 'Stomp Out the Fires of My Heart.' Cheney got all the fucking credit, man, but we was the ones who wrote it. Cheney wrote the flip side, 'Lost and Found Love.' You got that? It was me and Frankie, y'hear. And if you find the prick, just tell him he owes me plenty. Fuckin' plenty."

And then Pitts ducked back into the hole he came from.

It was ancient history, as far as I was concerned. The world wasn't going to change just because someone got credit for something he didn't do. It happens all the time. But it was the first bad word I'd heard about Janus since I'd started on the case, and it made me wonder if there were any other chinks in the knight's armor. Oddly enough, it made me feel good. Finally, it seemed like I was starting to scratch beneath the surface. Drugs, screwing your partners, now we were getting somewhere.

I left Mount Olympus with the sound of Pitts still raving about a song I'd never even heard of before still ringing in my ears. But I was worried about other things. The investigation was taking a direction I didn't expect: drugs, Mexico, the Peking Man, pyramids, and some mysterious Latin American Indian named Eagle Eyes. A guy gets iced in some Times Square sleaze-hole and I wind up taking a trip through the history of man. It seemed that, somehow, I'd managed to get myself involved in one giant crossword puzzle, and the clues to the theme of the puzzle just didn't seem to make any sense. And I had the nagging feeling that I was over my head, way over my head. ✿

# Sharp
## REVELATIONS

I DROVE EAST ON SUNSET, through Beverly Hills, headed in the direction where I thought the Hollywood freeway ought to be. Glancing in my rearview mirror, I noticed a large black sedan behind me. I weaved in and out of traffic, but it seemed to stick to my tail. I took a couple of quick, sharp turns and wound up almost losing my way on the dark, unfamiliar streets. When I finally resurfaced on Sunset, the black sedan was still hugging my rear end. So much for private eye stunts.

The car was carrying two people, anonymous in the shadows. I slowed down to get a better look, but the driver switched on his brights and I was momentarily blinded by the light reflected in my rear mirror.

Fifteen minutes later, just before my carriage was due to turn into a pumpkin, I reached the hotel. I got out of the car, flipped the attendant a five spot, and watched as my wheels burned rubber in the direction of the parking lot. Looking back toward the street, I spotted the black sedan slowing down as it approached the hotel. My chaperone on the passenger's side gave me a hard look. I was worried, but I didn't want to show it, so I gave him a friendly wave and blew him a kiss. He leaned over and said something to the driver and then, with Cinderella tucked safely in for the night, the automobile sped away.

The next morning, I got up early, showered, shaved, dressed and headed down to the lobby to wait for Jack Sharp. It was nine-thirty and Sharp was due at ten. I bought a paper, found a seat facing the hotel entrance, then sat back and read what was happening in the real world. Buried three quarters of the way down on page ten, I ran into an item of particular interest.

### Former Rock Star Dies in Freak Accident

The last known member of a once famed rock and roll group died here today in the final episode in a series of bizarre tragedies which has claimed the lives of several members of the one-time pop group, Jason and the Argonauts. Mike Pitts, 42, died instantly last night when a large chunk of a facade, apparently carried by last night's strong winds, blew from a building and struck Pitts on the head. Pitts, a former member of the group which soared to fame in the early 1980s with the hit single, 'Stomp Out the Fires of My Heart,' had been appearing at Mount Olympus in Marina del Ray with a group calling itself Zeus. He was evidently walking toward his car when the accident occurred. The only member of the group still unaccounted for, Jason Cheney, the leader of Jason and the Argonauts, disappeared nearly 15 years ago and is presumed dead.

A chill went down my back. I tore the item out, folded it up, and put it in my pocket. Coincidence? I didn't think so. Some people will argue life is made up of a series of unconnected coincidences. I'm not one of them. But then that's understandable, because if that's the way life is, just a series of unrelated coincidences, guys like me who make their living putting things together, solving puzzles, would be out of business. No, the world's got to be a little more reasonable, logical and schematic than that. I'm not saying that ultimately everything makes sense, but I am saying the chances are if a series of events look like they're connected, they usually are. All you've got to do to make sense out of them is make the right connections, join the dots, and come up with the full picture. Of course, if you mess up on one of those connections, you're done for. That's why you've got to be so careful, so methodical. It's tough, sometimes frustrating work, but it's what I do and I try to do it the best I can.

The only danger I'd ever faced before was from someone carrying a baseball bat, or throwing foreign objects at me or, at the worst, someone trying to throw a punch. Somehow I'd always managed to move fast enough and avoid injury. Not anymore. Either I'd slowed down or I was now playing in the big leagues and maybe I just wasn't up to the challenge.

Jack Sharp walked into the lobby.

"How ya doing, Mr. Swann?" Sharp called out, waving his hand in greeting. He looked different. It took a minute for me to realize it was his hair. It was styled differently. I looked closer. He was wearing a toupee. A good one. He smiled at me with a mouth full of store-bought teeth. In fact, there didn't seem to be very much real about Jack Sharp, making him perfect for Hollywood, I thought.

"You're looking better today," Sharp said.

"A good night's sleep will do that for you, I guess." He extended his hand. I took it. It was limp and damp. "What was it you wanted to see me about?"

"We'll eat, then talk. They've got a great little coffee shop here."

"I guess you're pretty familiar with this hotel, huh?"

"What do you mean?"

"Well, you were here last night, weren't you? I thought I saw you talking to someone."

He shook his head. "No, you must be mistaken. I wasn't here last night. In fact, I haven't been in this hotel for months."

"My mistake," I said, and maybe it was.

I had juice and coffee while Sharp ordered a plate of sunny-side up eggs, potatoes and toast. I picked the seeds out of my orange juice and sipped coffee impatiently as Sharp, soaking up the yolks of his eggs with a wedge of buttered toast, talked about everything in the damn world but the reason for his visit. Finally, he edged closer and I knew we were going to get down to brass tacks.

"It's a very interesting business you're in, Mr. Swann. I've never met a real detective before. I'm afraid my impression was formed, like everyone else's I suppose, by movies and TV. How did you get into the business, if you don't mind my asking?"

"Just lucky, I guess."

"Hmm, well I guess luck can only take you so far in this world." Sharp smiled. I didn't like it. It was crooked, which he probably couldn't help, but I still couldn't cut him any slack.

"How far has it taken you?"

His eyebrows raised. "Not as far as I'd hoped, I'm afraid. But you never know when luck is going to strike, do you?"

"No, you don't."

"What sort of cases do you normally handle, Mr. Swann?"

"Repos, divorces, collections, lost husbands...."

"Not very glamorous, is it?"

"Certainly not as glamorous as the silver screen."

"Then this sort of case is new for you. I hope you're not in over your head."

"I hope so too, Mr. Sharp. But you know something, over the years I've learned how to be a pretty good swimmer." I didn't really believe this, of course, but I hoped Sharp did.

"What would you say was your most interesting or bizarre case?"

"Are we talking movie material here?"

"I'm just interested."

"Well, since you asked, they're all on the odd side. People don't come to me for help unless something out of the ordinary has happened. If they led normal lives, they wouldn't need me. If people didn't cheat on their spouses, welsh on their debts, neglect their responsibilities, steal from their neighbors, in short, if they stopped being human beings, then I guess I'd probably be selling haberdashery somewhere. Fortunately, I'm pretty sure there'll always be more than enough work for guys like me."

Wiping up the remainder of his eggs with the last slice of toast, then following it up with a bacon chaser, Sharp said, "I suppose you're wondering what I wanted to see you about."

"The thought crossed my mind."

Sharp smiled and sucked at his teeth. "It's about Cheney, of course. I thought you ought to know I met with him a couple of months ago." Sharp paused and smiled again. He pushed his plate away and watched me closely, for my reaction, I assumed.

"Here in L.A.?"

"He came out here to talk to me about something."

"What?"

"Look, Swann, Carole doesn't know anything about this. He called me at the studio and said he had to see me. That it was important. He said he needed my help. I'd never even met the man before. He was long gone by the time Carole and I got together. All I knew about him was what she told me and that wasn't much. I thought he was a shit for leaving her like that."

Sharp broke off and looked for the waitress. Spotting her by the counter, he waved her over and said, "How about another cup of coffee here, honey? How about you, Swann?"

"I'm fine."

"We met in my office at the studio. He wasn't at all what I'd expected. Carole always raved about how 'cool' he was, how together. But that day he had a weird look in his eyes, like a wild animal. At first, I couldn't understand what the hell he was talking about. I figured he was high on something. It came down to him wanting money. Financing for some project he was involved in."

"What project?"

Sharp grinned. The waitress arrived with a pot of coffee. Sharp patted her behind. "Thanks, honey." She smiled and bowed slightly.

"That's the weird part," Sharp continued, stirring his coffee. "You know, archaeology isn't my strong suit, so I don't know why the hell he came to me. I mean money I got, but not for every harebrained scheme that comes my way. What I'm saying is, I'm no soft touch. Anyway, he starts telling me this whole involved story about these lost bones and how important they are to mankind, that they're worth a fortune to the man who finds them and that scientists would give their eye teeth to get hold of them. He says he has a sure lead on where to find them, but he needs a lot of money to finish the search. So I asked him, why come to me? He says, 'Because there's no one else I can turn to.' What made him think he could turn to me, I don't know. In any case, he intimated that if I didn't cooperate he might make trouble for me."

"What kind of trouble?"

"Beats me. Listen, Swann," he said earnestly, leaning forward so that his face was only inches from mine, "I don't scare easy. If he wanted money or anything else for that matter, that was the wrong way to get it from me."

"What else did he tell you?"

"That he was looking for something called the Peking Man. Know any thing about it?"

"Nope."

"Well, all I know is what Cheney told me, so that's what I'll tell you. Seems that in the late '20s some Austrian geologist named Otto something or other dug up some weird looking skeletons near some hill called, well, I think it was called Dragon Bone Hill, or something like that, in China. Anyway, scientists checked them out and found they were legit, apparently the remains of some prehistoric race. Cheney claimed they were some sort of crucial link in man's development.

"Anyway, they called the bones Peking Man and kept digging. I think they came up with parts of at least forty more of these Peking Men, but the war was coming and then, it was somewhere around 1941, they decided that the medical school in Peking, where they'd been keeping the fossils, was no longer safe. Some Marine Lieutenant, a guy named Foley, claimed the bones were then taken to the home of his commander, named Ashurst, and put into Marine footlockers. Later, they were taken to Camp Holcomb, a Marine outpost at the foot of the Great Wall. But before they could be shipped to the States, the Japs captured the base. Ashurst and Foley managed to hold on to one of the lockers during most of their time in a Jap prison camp, but by the time Foley got out in 1945, the footlocker had disappeared. Since then there's been no trace of the bones."

Sharp paused and sipped his coffee. I thought it rather odd that he knew the story so well, especially for someone who'd feigned disinterest in Cheney's plans. Truth is, I might have doubted the whole story if Pitts hadn't mentioned the Peking Man the night before.

"Cheney said all kinds of leads have turned up since the war, but the bones have never been found. Some years ago, as a matter of fact, some Chicago stockbroker named Christopher Janus offered five hundred grand for information leading to the recovery of the bones. In June of '72, he received a call from some woman with a deep German accent who claimed she was the widow of a Marine who'd been stationed in China during the war. She said she had a footlocker full of bones that her husband had left her. She lived back east, and Janus offered to meet her in New York. She suggested the top of the Empire State Building. She said she had to be careful because her husband warned her that the bones were dangerous, bad karma, you know, and that two people had already been killed because of them. So, they agreed to meet on the observation deck on the last Friday in June. When they met she showed him a photograph of an open footlocker with some fossils in it. She said she'd give them up for the five hundred grand. Just then a tourist aimed a camera in her direction. She got spooked and ran off. It was the last time he ever saw her, but he did get one more phone call from her. She told him she was frightened and that he'd have to deal with her lawyer. A few days later, some guy calling himself Harrison Seng got in touch with Janus. Said he was a lawyer working for the German woman. Janus had Seng checked out after their conversation and there was no record of anyone by that name being a lawyer."

I sipped my now-cold coffee.

"Are you still with me, Henry?" Sharp asked, as if I were some kind of idiot. I hate when someone who hardly knows me calls me Henry. It suggests a kind of intimacy that pisses me off. Sharp pissed me off, in more ways than one, but I tried hard not to show it.

"Yes, Jack, I'm with you."

"Great. Anyway, Seng sent Janus the photo and he had it examined by an expert who found it was very possibly authentic. Seng told Janus he wanted assurances from Uncle Sam that his client would not be prosecuted. Janus checked and found that the statute of limitations had run out, so she was safe. Unfortunately, though, the Chinese weren't so willing to forgive and forget. By this time they wanted those fossils back real bad. No immunity, no bones, and that's the way it stood when Cheney approached me. He told me there had been other leads, but none panned out. Up to now every street's been a dead end, but Cheney was sure the German broad was telling the truth, that she had the bones. He was determined to find her and the bones. But for that he needed..." Sharp rubbed his fingers together.

"Did you give it to him?"

"Mr. Swann, I'm a businessman, not a fool. As far as I was concerned, it was a wild goose chase. I wasn't interested in sinking any of my hard-earned cash into a fairy tale. I didn't doubt his sincerity, you understand, but I did doubt his ability to lay his hands on those bones. He said he could locate them, but he wouldn't say how. I couldn't be expected to trust him, could I?"

Sharp smiled and took another sip of coffee. I didn't trust him. But that's nothing new. I don't trust anyone. No one tells the whole truth. There's always something added or left out. What I had to do was figure out just how much truth there was in this story. The truth is a funny thing. You can tell a little of it and you can make the rest look real. But once you've fiddled with the truth, you've ruined it forever. All you're left with is the illusion of truth, which can be very dangerous. I knew that was what Sharp was doing, but it was up to me to extract what truth I could from the lies I believed he was spinning. It wouldn't be easy.

"I don't understand why he came to you."

Sharp shrugged. "Money's a helluva magnet, Swann. He knew I had dough and thought he could pry some loose."

"From what I understand, he had money of his own."

"Never count anyone else's money, Swann. This town is a perfect example. You look at the way some of these people live and you'd swear they got bucks comin' out the wazoo, but check out their creditors and you'll find the truth is very different."

"What did he do when you refused him the money?"

"He got up and left. He didn't even ask about Carole. Like he couldn't have cared less. You don't think those bones had anything to do with his death, do you?"

"I don't know," I said, and it was true, though I would have said it anyway. "I suppose it's possible," I said, toying with my spoon, twirling it in tiny, concentric circles on the table.

"I'm surprised we didn't hear about his death out here. After all, he was a celebrity of sorts."

"He wasn't Jason Cheney anymore."

"What do you mean?"

"He went by another name. Harry Janus."

"Janus? Do you think there's any connection with that

stockbroker fellow from Chicago?"

"Could be just a coincidence," I said, though, of course, I didn't believe that for a second.

"You think so? Well, if you ask me, Cheney's death had something to do with those damn bones. He probably got mixed up with the wrong element."

"Listen, Sharp, you were in the music business, weren't you?"

"For about a minute and a half, something I would prefer to forget. You wouldn't believe what a crazy racket it is. I couldn't stomach the kind of people I was expected to deal with."

"How come you didn't know Cheney when he was Cheney?"

"It's a big business, Swann," he said. "There are a lot of people I never met."

"You knew Mike Pitts, though."

"Mike Pitts?"

"Yeah. He said he knew you."

"Oh, yes. Mike Pitts."

"So you did know him?"

"The name's familiar."

"Yeah, I'm sure it is. How'd you know him?"

"Well, if it's the Mike Pitts I'm thinking of, he's in the music business and I think I steered him toward a couple of jobs."

"That's the one. And why did you help him find work?"

"Because he was a pretty good musician and he needed the work."

"How altruistic of you."

"I'm a very charitable man, Swann."

"When did you see him last?"

"God, it must be years. I didn't even know he was still alive."

"Funny thing about that, he's not."

"Really?"

"Yup. Died last night, as a matter of fact. Not long after I met up with him."

"Well, Swann, I hope you've got an alibi."

"You know, as fate would have it, I don't. I guess I may be in some trouble, huh?"

Sharp looked at his watch. "Well, it's getting rather late. I've got to get back to the studio. You know, this may seem strange, but are you certain Cheney is dead?"

"That is strange. Why do you ask?"

"Oh, I don't know," he said, waving his hand in the air. "It just occurred to me that if a man has had two identities in his life, well then, why not a third? Or even a fourth?"

"Why not indeed?"

"Then it occurred to you, too?"

"No, it didn't actually, because he is dead."

"You can be sure?"

"Yes."

"You saw the body?"

"No. But there was a positive identification."

"Ah, well. Just a thought. Will you be in L.A. much longer?"

"Not much reason to be, is there?"

Sharp smiled, because, I assumed, I'd told him what he wanted to hear. "I suppose not," he said. "I really don't think you'll find anything more out here. Your answer, if there is one, is probably back east."

Sharp paid the tab. I didn't even make a show of reaching for my wallet. It was his party and he'd pay if wanted. We got up from the table. He moved beside me and put his arm on my shoulder. It gave me the creeps, but I didn't make a move to push him away.

We parted company outside the coffee shop. I waited for the elevator and watched Sharp stop for a moment and speak to two men who'd just entered the hotel. He spoke animatedly, touching them gently on their arms and shoulders. They were still talking when I got into the elevator, and for some reason I thought of Louis Leakey and the origin of man.

# The Whole Truth
## AND NOTHING BUT...

I'D HARDLY GOT THE KEY OUT OF THE DOOR when the telephone rang. I picked it up to hear a tentative voice whispering, "Swann?"

"Yeah. Who is this? I can hardly hear you."

The voice, a little louder, said, "It's Carole Sharp. I have to see you. Right away."

"Why's that?"

There was a moment's hesitation. "I'm scared half out of my mind. Can you come right over? Please?" The last word was punctuated by a low, guttural sound that might have been a sob, though it sounded more like it came from a wounded animal, certainly not from the temptress I'd traded wisecracks with the day before.

Before I could reply, there was the sound of air being sucked in, as if through a straw in an empty glass, and Carole Sharp asked, "Have you seen this morning's paper?"

"Yes."

"Did you read about Mike Pitts?"

"Yeah."

Her voice became more frantic. "I'm afraid…"

"Of what?"

"Afraid…I'm next…I have no one…to turn to."

I switched the receiver to my other ear, sat down at the edge of the bed, and began twisting the phone cord around my free hand. "How about your husband?"

"That's impossible," she said, with a hint of irritation.

"Why's that?"

"Please, there's no time to discuss this now."

"Okay, I'll be right over. Just lock all the doors and don't open them for anybody but me. And keep that damn dog inside the house with you."

"All right," she said, a sudden calmness entering her voice. "Please hurry, though."

Fifteen minutes later I'd parked my car two blocks from the Sharp home, just to make sure I wasn't followed. I pounded on the front door in near perfect harmony with the barking of the dog. I heard padded footsteps, then a small, frightened voice asked, "Who is it?"

"Swann. Open up or I'll blow your house down."

There was the sound of several locks opening, a chain fell and the door opened slowly. A bloodshot eye peered out. I stepped into its path and only then did the door open wide enough for me to enter.

The door slammed shut behind me and the room echoed with the sound of closing locks. It sounded like a Medeco convention and I had the thought that maybe it was to keep me in rather than someone else out. Brutus barked loudly, his teeth bared menacingly as he made a move toward me. Cheney gave the animal a quick hand signal and he backed off, making a low growling sound under his breath. "Nice doggie," I said, holding my hands in front of me in a sign of peace.

Through a small opening in the draperies a beam of light fell on Mrs. Sharp. She was not the same woman I'd met the day before. Dressed in an old housecoat, her stringy hair was in such disarray that she looked more like Medusa than Monroe.

I led the way into the living room. The shades were drawn tight and the lights were off. I stumbled over something hard in the dark, performed a dandy little pirouette, caught my balance and cursed softly. "How about some light in here?"

"I thought it would be safer with them off," she replied. "Maybe they'd think no one was home."

"Who's they?"

She shook her head and her hair, tangled and matted, dropped in front of her eyes. She brushed it away. She was nervous. Her body, yesterday taut and firm, was loose and trembling. Her arms were wrapped tightly around her chest as though she were holding herself together by the dint of sheer physical might. I couldn't decide whether she was really frightened or whether it was all an act for my benefit. I switched on a lamp next to the sofa and asked, "Where's the booze?"

"Over there," she said, gesturing to the far corner of the room.

I found a bottle of scotch, poured three-fingers worth, and handed it to her. "Drink this."

"I don't want—"

"Drink it," I ordered. Her hands trembled. The glass shook. She brought it to her mouth. In one quick, smooth motion, she threw her head back and drained the glass. She choked, coughed twice, then wiped her mouth with the back of her hand. I poured myself a shot. "Okay," I said. "Now get a grip on yourself. Sit down and tell me what this is all about. And no lies. Everything on the table."

We sat on the couch, a few inches apart, facing the fireplace. Cheney leaned forward, flicked a hidden switch on the underside of the coffee table, and suddenly a fire roared in front of us. "I like it, do you mind?" she asked. "It relaxes me."

Above the fireplace, Jason Cheney's gold record caught the light from the lamp and reflected it back on us. I had to shift my position on the couch slightly when the light began hurting my eyes.

"Go ahead," I said.

"They're all gone now," she whimpered, her voice losing all its bite of the day before. Rendered harmless now, it trailed off into nothingness near the end of the sentence, her words lost somewhere inside her.

"If you want my help you'll have to do a lot better than that, or else I'm walking."

"No, don't," she said, grabbing my sleeve. I touched her hand. It was cold and clammy. "Everyone in the group is dead now. You know it's no coincidence."

"But you weren't in the group, were you? So, even if it is something more sinister, you don't have any thing to worry about."

"Anyone that had anything to do with Jason or that damn group of his is dead now. I'm next. I know it."

"Rock and roll is here to stay," I muttered. She looked at me. I was going to say, sorry, but I didn't. Instead, I watched her hands. I was fascinated by their movement. She didn't seem to know what to do with them, yet their path was smooth, graceful, belying the tension she appeared to be under. It was bizarre, as if they had a mind, a life, a language of their own. First they were neatly folded in her lap, a moment later she was nervously wringing them together. Then she touched her face and combed her tangled hair with them. A moment later they rested peacefully on her knees. Only when they touched me did they lose their animation. Those hands bothered me. They seemed to be out of synch with the what she was saying and, even worse, how she was supposedly feeling.

"Why?" I asked, still hypnotized by her hands, which now gently caressed her leg.

"I don't know."

"Think about it," I said sternly. I knew there was something to be said and I wanted to get it out of her.

She hesitated another moment before she said, "I didn't tell you every thing yesterday...."

"Really?"

"I know that Jason was in L.A. recently. Jack saw him. I don't know what it was about, though."

"How did you find out?"

"I saw a note in Jack's datebook—about a meeting."

"You didn't ask him about it?"

"No."

"I don't see how this translates into danger for you."

"Wouldn't you be frightened if you were me?"

"I'm frightened and I'm not you. But I'm still not sure what all this has to do with you."

"I think maybe Jason and Jack were in some kind of business together."

"What kind of business?"

"I don't know."

I looked into Carole Sharp's eyes. She looked back at me and held my gaze. I couldn't be sure, but I thought, if this chick's acting, she's doing an Academy Award performance. So maybe I was getting closer to the truth, but I was still a far cry from being all the way there. After all, there were those phone calls she'd made to Janus in New York, so I knew she had to know about his name change.

"Did you know he saw your husband and asked him for money, too?"

"Jack never said anything about that. You're not making this up, are you?"

"Listen, honey, I'm not the one who's good at making up stories."

"Are you accusing me of lying?"

"You've never lied to me before, so why should I believe you would now? Let's talk about Mexico."

"I don't know what you mean."

"Your ex-husband's trip to Mexico."

She had a blank look on her face. I got up, but before I could get far, she jumped up from the couch and pleaded with me. "No, please, wait. Come back. I'll tell you."

I sat back down. Frankly, I still had a feeling I was being set up, but I wanted to believe I was in control of the situation. While Carole remained silent a moment, presumably constructing the tale she was going to tell me, I stared at the flickering light coming from the plastic logs. Expecting heat from the phony fireplace, it gave off only light; but the light was a strange, otherworldly orange color, illuminating little, instead giving everything in the room an eerie orange tint. The breeze from the air-conditioning vent directly overhead gently ruffled my hair. I couldn't seem to shake a feeling of artificiality, the feeling I was just a character in someone else's movie.

"Okay, let's get started," I said impatiently. I wanted to get out of there, out of that house, that city, back to where I belonged.

Carole Sharp glared at me. "Jason was down in Mexico after he left me. In the beginning, he called me a few times, but he didn't say much. Small talk. About the divorce. Like that. He never told me what he was doing down there, but I know he was a real freak about those Aztec ruins. He was fascinated by anything old. He had dozens of books on archaeology and anthropology. He was a nut about it. He was always taking these weekend trips down there whenever he could get away. He said if he had his way, he'd go to Egypt some day and spend the rest of his life studying the pyramids, searching for Amhotep's tomb, or going to Africa on a dig. He had this thing about an archaeologist named Leakey. He was always talking about him, like he was some kind of God. Anyway, after three or four months, I didn't hear from him again. It was like he'd been swallowed up by the earth. Nothing. Not even a lousy postcard. From that time until a few weeks ago, I didn't know anything about Jason Cheney. For all I knew, he died years ago."

"How do you explain his fascination for that stuff ?"

"I can't...really...but one day he did tell me that the only way to understand ourselves was to understand our history. How we got here. What made us what we were. He used to drag me to museums, where he'd stare at these artifacts. He once told me that if he ever made a lot of money, that's what he'd do with it. Buy stuff like that and start a private collection. But I didn't pay any attention to him."

"Maybe you should have. How did he plan to get that kind of money?"

"I have no idea. To me, it was just a lot of idle talk."

"Another thing that seems to crop up in this investigation again is drugs."

"I don't know anything about that," she said a little too quickly. "And Jason wouldn't have had any thing to do with that."

"You're such a good judge of character, huh? And what about Jack?"

"No."

"Did he know Jason back then?"

"No."

"You're sure? Because that's not what Pitts told me last night."

"I don't care what Mike Pitts told you," she said angrily. Suddenly, her eyes regained some of their past sparkle and her face drew color. "Jack definitely did not know Jason. You can't believe everything that dopehead tells you."

"When did Cheney leave you?"

"The spring of '83, and he didn't leave me. I kicked him the hell out."

"Why was that?"

"Because he was an asshole."

"That's not what I've been hearing about him."

"You didn't live with him like I did."

"No, I didn't. Why'd you kick him out?"

"Because he cheated on me, that's why."

"How'd you find out?" I asked, secretly pleased that I was finding out that Janus wasn't all he'd been cracked up to be.

"I didn't have to be a genius to know he was playing around. He was a rock musician, for Chrissakes."

"So you never actually caught him in the act?"

"I didn't have to. Besides, he was happy to leave. It gave him the chance to go down to Mexico, and that's what he wanted."

"Do you know where he stayed while he was in Mexico?"

"He was in Mexico City for a while, but the last time I heard from him he was in Acapulco."

"Where'd he stay?"

"Some hotel."

"Well now, that's a big help. Which one?"

"You expect me to remember?"

"Yeah, well, I was hoping to get lucky."

She gave me an exasperated look. "Maybe it was the El Presidente. But he was only there a couple weeks. He moved out. But it wasn't another hotel. Somewhere outside the city."

"Got an address?"

"You must be kidding. After all these years?"

"Well, who was he staying with?"

"I don't know...some guy he either met down there or knew from before."

"Was his name Eagle Eyes?"

"Yeah, that's it."

"I still can't figure out why someone would want you all dead."

"There is no reason." Her eyes teared up. I moved closer and put my arm around her. She stiffened, then began to cry.

"Look, if someone wanted to kill you, they'd have done it long ago. It doesn't make sense to wait this long. Whatever's going on, I don't think you're part of it."

"So what is going on?"

"I don't know...that's what I'm here for. To find out."

"Stay here with me awhile," she pleaded, in a voice that suddenly turned sexy. "I don't want to be alone."

"You've got the dog. And if you're so worried, why not just call up your husband. In fact, I don't know why you didn't call him in the first place."

She hesitated a moment. A glazed look came over her face. "He wouldn't understand. He thinks I've got an overactive imagination. He'd just think I was being melodramatic."

"Well?"

"Well what?"

"Are you?"

Her face turned hard, her eyes cold. "They're all dead, aren't they? I didn't make that up, did I?"

"Look, I'm just trying to make some sense out of all this. I speak to five different people and I get half a dozen different stories. I don't know what to believe anymore."

"You believe me, don't you?" she asked, putting her hand on my thigh.

"Should I?"

"Of course. Why would I lie?

"All this is kind of new to me. I'm used to chasing after cars and bail jumpers, not dead men. So give me a break, will ya?"

She reached forward and toyed with the fireplace switch, turning it on and off a couple of times.

It was time to go. I wasn't going to get any thing else accomplished here, and the last thing I wanted to do was run into Jack Sharp again. "I've got to get going," I said.

Cheney moved closer. She played with the fireplace switch with her foot. She ran her finger across my cheek. She leaned forward and kissed me on the mouth. "You don't really have to go right now, do you? What are you going to do now? Where will you go?" she asked, making fists out of her small hands. Her knuckles turned white.

"I think I'll take a little trip down south," I said. ✦

# Strange
## BEDFELLOWS

THE BLACK SEDAN WAS BACK. Parked across from my car, the sinister looking car's engine turned over—a soft purring sound in a machine built for speed—and cruised away just as I turned the corner and stepped into view. I ran into the middle of the road in hopes of catching the plate number. No luck. The California plate was obscured by mud, though, I noted, it hadn't rained as long as I'd been west.

I got into my car and headed back toward the hotel. My fingers thumped nervously on the steering wheel. I switched on the radio and flipped the dial from one station to the next. The music jangled my nerves, so I shut it off. I had this funny feeling in the pit of my stomach. It was the kind of fear that made you want to run and hide.

Turning onto the freeway, I caught sight of the black sedan again out of the corner of my eye. It had doubled back and was on my trail again. My heart sped up and I pressed down harder on the accelerator. My car lurched forward, but the black sedan mirrored my move and did me one better, closing the gap between us. Soon, the black sedan filled my rearview mirror. Realizing I was woefully outgunned, I lifted my foot slightly from the gas pedal and my car slowed. The black sedan slowed also. No use trying to lose it, I thought.

ACK IN MY ROOM, I peered out over the balcony at the black sedan now parked by the curb near the hotel. I could make out two men seated in the front. I shut the curtain and called the Mexican Embassy and arranged for a visitor's permit, which I was told I could pick up the next day.

The telephone rang. It was Sally Janus. "Henry, thank God I finally got you."

"How'd you find me?"

"I tried every damn hotel in L.A., that's how. Don't you think you could have called and let me know you were all right?"

"I was busy."

"You seem to forget that you're working for me."

"I haven't forgotten."

"I think I'm entitled to a progress report."

"I've got some leads."

"Like what?"

"Your husband was a very interesting man."

"I know that. That's not what I'm paying you to find out. What about that woman? Did you see her?"

"Yes."

"Who is she?"

"She was married to Harry."

"What?"

"Fifteen years ago…he had another name, another life."

"My God!" She was silent a moment. "Does she know anything about his murder?"

"I don't think so, but you know, she did look awfully

familiar to me."

"How could you have possibly met her before."

"I couldn't have. I'm sure it's just one of those things."

"What else did you find out?"

"I found out he spent some time in Mexico. I'd like to go down there for a day or two to check out some things."

"What things?"

"There are all these leads and they all seem to point in different directions. Frankly, I'm a little confused. I've got to get myself back on track and I think a trip down there can do that. It's your dough. I can stop now, if you like."

She was silent. I wondered what she was thinking. Finally, she said, "All right. I'll give you two days. But that's it."

"Do me a favor. Go to my apartment. I'll call ahead and the super will let you in. Slip him a couple of bucks and add it to my expenses. In my top dresser drawer, under my socks, you'll find my passport. FedEx it out here, will you?"

"Suddenly I've become your assistant?"

I gave her my address, then asked, "How did your husband leave you financially?"

"Why do you ask?"

"Because it's important."

"Not as much as I thought. Evidently, he went through a lot of his capital in the last six months—he was even in the midst of trying to refinance the house. I didn't know all this until I spoke to our lawyer. I'm going to sell the house, and there's plenty of equity there, and there's some jewelry—so you don't have to worry about your fee."

"Believe me, I'm not worried. But I'm going to need some more money for travel expenses. I'm running low."

"How much?"

"A couple thousand ought to do it."

"Swann, don't treat me like an ATM." She hesitated a moment. "All right. But I want you to call me and tell me what you've found."

I wondered how far I could push this. And then I wondered, again, why Sally Janus was so dead-set on finding her husband's killer. I had the distinct feeling that once her husband died, the money train had run off the track, so what did she possibly have to gain by throwing good money after bad?

I showered and then, as I was removing clothing from my bag, I noticed my pistol. I clicked the chamber open. I removed six bullets from a plastic baggie I'd stashed in the side pocket of the bag. I loaded the gun, snapped the chamber shut and stuck the weapon in my belt on the right side. I didn't like the idea of carrying a loaded revolver—I'd never even used it outside the shooting range—but I was afraid I might need it.

There was a knock at the door. I put on my jacket and buttoned it to conceal the weapon.

"Who is it?"

"Room service."

"I didn't order any thing. You must have the wrong room."

"It's a telegram, sir, and you'll have to sign for it."

I opened the door a crack to see who it was. As soon as I did, I felt a weight push hard against it, smashing the door against me and throwing me back ward into the room. Before I could regain my balance, two men rushed in and one, a giant of a man, well over six feet and weighing maybe 300 grabbed me in a bear hug and pushed me toward the edge of the bed.

"What the hell…" I sputtered, entrapped in the big man's arms. I tried to escape, but the big man was too strong. He loosened his grip for a moment, grabbed my arms, then twisted them tight behind my back.

"Shut up and nothing too bad'll happen," the second man growled. He was smaller than the first, somewhere under five-five, and while he spoke, the big man, his hand at the back of my neck, expertly slipping me into a full nelson, so I couldn't even twitch a muscle. The door slammed shut and the big man, his free hand moving down my side, said, "The dude's packin' heat."

The small man, his eyes hidden behind a pair of mirrored

sunglasses identical to a pair which hid the eyes of his bigger partner, frowned, then moved forward to slip the pistol from my belt. He pointed the gun in my face. "Naughty, naughty," he said lightly, then rammed his fist into my gut, then into my face, his ring tearing away a piece of flesh from just under my right eye. I cried out in pain. The big man laughed, loosening his grip momentarily. I could feel my body jerk spasmodically in rhythm with his laugh.

"Just a sample," the small man said, massaging his knuckles lovingly. He sneered and, expecting another blow, I flinched. The big man laughed again, tightening his grip around my neck, forcing my eyes to the floor. Gasping for air, I felt the blood running down my face. I hoped it felt worse than it was. The small man nodded once and the big man released his grip, pushing me down onto the bed.

"Let's talk," the small man said, pulling a chair up to the bed. The big man, his face expressionless, arms folded in front of his massive chest, moved behind his partner. I touched my face gingerly and felt the warm blood trickling into my mouth.

"Don't worry about that. I've seen worse," the small man jeered, his face twisted into a sinister smile as he waved my gun in my face. Tasting blood, I grabbed for the bedsheet and held it to my face.

"You'll live," said the little man, "if you play ball. You got a big nose, Mr. Swann, and you're stickin' it where it don't belong. Understand?"

I nodded, still pressing the sheet firmly to my cheek. I was dazed and weak. My stomach was queasy. Blood was spilling from the open wound under my eye and some of it landed on my pants. Spreading, it deposited darkening reddish brown splotches on my clothing. A section of the bedsheet was turning scarlet. Losing all that blood frightened me.

"Swann," the little man said, turning the word over on his tongue. "What kind of name is that? French, maybe? You a frog, Swann?"

The big man laughed. "Or maybe it's German. Kraut name? Heinie? *Sprechen sie Deutsches*, maybe?"

"I didn't say anything. I was much too worried about my face. The big man said, "Swann, maybe like in Swannee River, Frankie. That's where he got his name, and maybe that's where he's gonna wind up if he don't cooperate. Right Frankie?"

The little man put his hand up in a gesture that quieted his partner.

"Well, see here, Mr. Swann, from wherever you're from, we have a certain friend who doesn't like the way you're conducting yourself here in L.A. He doesn't like the company you're keeping, if you get my drift. He thinks everyone ought to mind their own business, keep their beaks where they belong. If you get my meaning. You do get my meaning, don't you, Mr. Swann?"

"Yes," I said softly, removing the sheet from my face. Gingerly, I touched my wound. The flow of blood had slowed. I put the sheet back to my face.

"You know, Mr. Swann, this here's a mighty dangerous little weapon," the small man said, patting the pistol. "You shouldn't ought to be carrying around something as dangerous as this. It might go off accidentally. Shoot your goddamn cock right off." He looked at his partner. "Isn't that right, Albert?"

Albert smiled and nodded agreeably.

"Now, Mr. Swann, back to business. My friend suggests you get on a plane, a train, a boat, a bus, or any other means of conveyance that suits you, and leave L.A. before something quite serious occurs. Do you get my meaning, Mr. Swann?"

"Do I know the gentleman?"

The small man's face turned hard. He turned to his partner again and shook his head in disgust. "Mr. Swann here likes to ask smartass questions that aren't good for his health, doesn't he, Albert?" The big man grinned and made a move toward me. I hunched up my body, put up my hand and said, "Certainly no disrespect was intended. You and your friend here don't like questions, I won't ask them."

"That, Mr. Swann, is a very intelligent response," the small man said. "I think we're starting to speak the same language." His face widened into a grin. "And I'm certain we will not need to have this kind of conversation again, will we?"

"Not if I can help it."

He smiled. "Yes, I do like that name of yours. Very mellifluous. Poetic, almost. You are aware, of course, of the mythological implications. Leda and the swan. Apollo and the swan. I believe it's written somewhere that the swan is supposed to sing beautifully just before he leaves this earth. Personally, I believe that's merely a myth, Mr. Swann, and yet, if you persist in making waves, I'm afraid we will be forced to find out if it's true about one Swann in particular. I suppose you will be checking out quite soon."

"My bags are packed," I said, pointing to my closed suitcase in the corner.

"Fine. Then Albert and myself will be leaving you so you may see to the necessary travel arrangements. I do hope we will not be visiting you again, though it has been a pleasure. You know, you really ought to put something on that cut under your eye. It's a nasty-looking thing."

The big man smiled. The small man rose form his chair, my pistol dangling casually from his finger. He twirled it around, cowboy style, and smiled sheepishly. "I apologize for the theatrics. I just couldn't resist. When in Holly wood, do as the Hollywood cowboys. In any case, I believe you won't have much use for this, so we'll just hold on to it for you. We'll be leaving now, but perhaps, before we do, we ought to leave something for you to remember us by. A souvenir. Albert?" He turned and nodded to his partner. Albert unfolded his massive arms and stepped toward me. Before I could raise my arms to protect myself, as if that would have done any good, he'd caught me by the shoulders and lifted me to my feet. I decided to go the Gandhi route. I went limp. I closed my eyes and waited for the blow. Albert did not disappoint me. The last thing I remembered was feeling the breeze from the motion of Albert's arm. The little man said, "Sleep tight, Mr. Swann," and a split second later, as a high-pitched wailing sound escaped from deep inside me, I felt a tremendous blow to my gut, and it was night. ⚔

# Exit
## TINSELTOWN

**M**Y HEAD, STILL SMARTING from Albert's blow, was swimming with questions. I was certain of only three things: Harry Janus was dead; I was in pain; and I'd better get the hell out of L.A. before this particular swan wound up crooning his last tune. Oh, one more thing I was also sure of: my two visitors were the same men who'd occupied the black sedan. But who'd sent them? And why? Was it because I was getting too close to solving Janus's murder? Was it a jealous spouse getting rid of his wife's paramour?

I'd leave L.A. all right, but not for New York. I was going to Mexico. I should have bailed out. After all, money and pride aren't everything. But I felt I was close, very close, and I didn't want to give up, especially now that I was mad and felt I had something to prove.

The next morning, I packed up my things and checked out of the hotel. I wanted to give the appearance of heeding the advice given me, just in case someone was watching. I left my bag at the desk and asked the clerk to contact the rental agency and have them pick up my car. I called a cab and had them pick me up two blocks from the hotel. I sneaked out the back and took the cab to the Mexican Embassy, where I picked up my visitor's permit. I called another cab and had it to take me to a motel, where I spent the night. The next morning, I went back to the hotel, picked up my bag and a FedEx package with a money order and my passport.

I arrived at LAX by noon and went straight to the American Airlines desk, where I asked several innocuous questions to make it look as if I were purchasing a ticket. Then, losing myself in a crowd, I stashed my bag in an airport locker and bought a ticket on Aeromexico. The flight was scheduled to leave 2:00.

Seated at the gate, I fingered the scab under my right eye. I got antsy, though, so for the next fifteen minutes or so, I made a lazy circle around the terminal, trying to sort things out while, at the same time, keeping an eye open for any familiar face, especially Frankie and Albert. Seeing none, I felt a little more at ease.

Just before it was time to board the plane, I began to feel disoriented, as if I were suddenly alone in the world, unanchored and floating free. It was a terrible feeling, a sense of vulnerability that left me almost trembling. I was tempted to get on a plane back to New York and forget the whole thing. But I'd come this far, so why turn back now? ⚹

**PART ❸**

# MEXICO
*Los Angeles to Acapulco, Mexico*

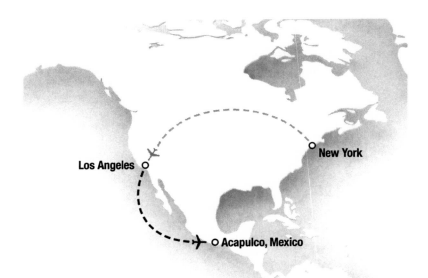

# ¿Donde Está AQUÍ?

STEPPING OFF THE PLANE IN ACAPULCO, I was greeted by a south of the border blast of hot air. By the time I'd climbed down the boarding ramp, my armpits were soaked and my hair curled from the humidity. Setting foot on foreign soil, I loosened my jacket, jauntily flinging it over my shoulder. It was good to be out of L.A., where the yellow air hung ominously overhead, discoloring the atmosphere and God knows what else. Here in Mexico, the air smelled and tasted better: fresher, less jaded. I was a new man. My spirits soared. My doubts disappeared.

Swallowing large hunks of baked air, I checked in at customs. I breezed through the standard questions, explaining I was in Mexico for a three-day holiday. It was late, the customs official looked beat and, since I had no baggage other than a small bag I stowed on the plane, I passed through quickly. Outside, I grabbed the first cab in line, an old, beat-up Ford, and asked the driver to take me to the El Presidente, which was, I figured, as good a place as any to start my search for Harry Janus's life in Mexico.

The driver, a dark-skinned Spanish-Indian, fortyish, with a thick black mustache, smiled, displaying several missing teeth, tipped his hat, a weatherworn straw job with a red band, said, "*Sí, señor,*" and the cab screeched off. Soon we were travelling up steep cliffs and maneuvering over winding roads. The old car, shockless, bounced furiously on the poorly paved highway, its brakes screeching sharply. The higher we climbed, the faster we went. The driver leaned forward, hat pushed back, his full concentration on the road ahead. Taking treacherous curves at forty and fifty miles an hour, the car occasionally swerved into the wrong lane. The moonlight cast frightening shadows onto the road ahead, only to disappear when the headlights shone on the spot of the black apparition. For the most part, though, the deep Mexican darkness hid all landmarks. After a while, I closed my eyes, held onto the strap over the window, and muttered a few Hail Marys. I didn't open them again until we'd slowed down in approach to the bright lights of the beach area.

We finally reached Costera Alemán, the Broadway of Acapulco. Hotels, restaurants and fancy condominiums, were lined up one after another in a horseshoe configuration semicircling the bay. Squeezed between a Holiday Inn and a condo was the El Presidente Hotel.

The driver stopped the car, twisted around and said, "Señor, *estamos aquí.* You need a guide, maybe? A girl? I know plenty. *Muy bonita.* They show you one *bueno tiempo.*"

I couldn't help but smile. "Cut the crap, Pancho. That stuff went out with the Cisco Kid. But if you want to make some *dinero, venga aquí a las neuve por la mañana.*" I said, in my best P.R. Spanish.

The driver removed his straw hat, wiped perspiration from his brow with a red bandana, and smiled. "Hey, man, you give the peoples what they want." He replaced his hat and bandana. "*Estaré aquí.* I get two and a half bucks an hour. That's American cash. We Mexicans are *muy perezosa*, man."

"It's a deal. See you tomorrow, Pancho, and be ready to earn your two and a half bucks."

The tourist season was over. It ended, for the most part, with the passing of Easter week, and now the hotels were nearly empty. Even without a reservation and despite the late hour, I had little trouble rustling up a room. Business was conducted swiftly and effortlessly with the well-dressed Spanish desk clerk who spoke impeccable English with the hint of a British accent. No baggage, no bellboy, so I had to find my own way up to my room. The clicking of my heels against the white marble floor magnified the eerie feeling that I was the only living soul in the hotel. I began to get the same feeling I'd had in the L.A. airport, a feeling of being alone. Only now it was alone in a strange country, engaged in a search that might be pointless, even fatal. Again, I had second thoughts. But again, I managed to fight them back. What I needed, I thought, was a good night's sleep. I held my finger on the elevator button until it finally swooshed open. Then I took it up to my room. 🕺

# El Gran
## ALEMÁN

THE NEXT MORNING, bright and early, still rubbing sleep out of my eyes, I spoke to the desk clerk, asking if the hotel had records dating back some fifteen years.

"I am sorry, señor, but we have no such records," he answered. "There is not the need. When the file is filled, we throw the cards away. And almost fifteen years ago, señor? *Todos de la tierra.*"

And so it goes with the happy-go-lucky Mexican, I thought, as I left the hotel, wondering about what I'd do next.

It was nine sharp, and when I looked across the boulevard, there was the old Ford. Walking in the bright morning sun, reflecting sharply off the white sidewalks, made my eyes ache. I put on my sunglasses. When I reached the cab, the driver, his head leaning back against the seat, a hat covering his face, was dozing at the wheel. I rapped on the roof of the car.

"Spend the night here?" I asked, getting as close to his ear as I could.

Slowly, he removed the straw hat from his face. "Ah, it is you, señor. *Buenos días.* I make a good impression, no?"

"Yeah, yeah, I'm impressed." I opened the back door of the cab and got in. The windows were closed, trapping the pungent aroma of Mexican food. I rolled down both windows.

"Where to, señor? The old marketplace to buy some silver? I would not let you get cheated, señor. I know just the right place.Very reliable. Very honest. He likes Americans. A Dodgers fan. Fernando Valenzuela is his all-time hero. Or maybe the morning beach to see all the *bonita señoritas*? Or the Lost City of the Pretty Ladies. This is a sight you will not want to miss, señor. You name it, I will take you there."

"Fine, but first I'm interested in some information. You lived here long?"

"All my life, señor. *Soy de aquí.* I know this city, *yo se esta ciudad completo.* As you say, like the back of my hand."

"Then maybe you can help me. I've come here to look for a man."

"You have come to the right one, señor. Man, woman, child, José *se conoce todos.*"

"How about a man named Jason Cheney. He would have been here a long time ago."

The driver removed his hat and scratched his head. "No, señor," he said. "That name means nothing to me. A *tourista,* maybe. They come and go like flies on a dog. I'm sorry."

"How about a man named Harry Janus?"

He smiled benignly and shrugged apologetically. "No, señor...I am sorry."

"How about someone named Eagle Eyes?"

His face lit up. "Ah, señor, him I know. He is what you call a real big shot around here. Señor Eagle Eyes knows *todo que pasa en Acapulco.* You want something, you go to Señor Eagle Eyes. Very powerful."

"Then that's the man I want to see. Take me to him."

We drove north, toward the hills of La Sabana, toward the

City of the Pretty Ladies. As José drove, I tracked our route on a road map I'd picked up at the hotel. The air breezed through the open windows, cooling the backseat and ridding the car of the stench of food. I was surprised at how easy it was to locate this Eagle Eyes. A bit of luck, for a change, I thought.

We traveled almost an hour into the hills, finally reaching a large clearing surrounded by a high iron gate. Set about a hundred yards back was a large white hacienda with a smaller house next to it. The area was thickly covered with lush greenery, trees and blooming flowers. In contrast to the dusty roads and rocky terrain we'd just come through, this was Paradise.

As we pulled up to the gate, José announced, "Señor Eagle Eyes does not like visitors. He is a strange man. There is a *telefono* at the gate. You will speak to him?"

"Sure," I said, opening the car door and getting out. It was very hot. Perspiration ran down my back. I walked to the gate and was surprised when I read the nameplate on the gate. Instead of Eagle Eyes, it read K. Egeleise. I smiled. Even words were playing tricks on me in this case. I picked up the phone and, a moment later, a voice said, "Si?"

"My name is Henry Swann," I said, in the best Spanish I could muster. "I've come to see Señor Egeleise."

A heavily accented voice replied in broken English, "Señor Egeleise sees no visitors. Go away."

"Tell him it concerns a man named Jason Cheney, and if that doesn't mean anything to him, try Harry Janus. I'll wait here for his answer."

Several moments passed. Finally, the voice returned. "Señor Egeleise will see you."

The gate buzzed and swung open. I stepped inside quickly. It closed behind me. "Wait for me," I shouted back at José, who was standing or rather leaning against the car. "I won't be long."

José waved half-heartedly, then got back in the car. The last I saw of him, he was leaning back against the seat in his dozing position, his face covered by his hat.

As I walked toward the house, an Indian, his face the color of copper, dressed in a white Mexican shirt embroidered in green and red with the sleeves rolled up, a thin black tie and black slacks, suddenly appeared beside me. "This way, señor," he said, taking me by the elbow. "Señor Egeleise will see you in his study."

I was led through a large foyer leading to a long hallway and then into the study. Three walls were lined with books. Against the fourth wall there was a glass encased gun rack. In a large leather chair sat a man, reading *The New York Times*. Wagner was playing softly in the background.

"Señor Egeleise, I presume," I said. "My name is Henry Swann and I'm here to ask you some questions."

Egeleise put down the paper, rose and extended his hand. White-haired, in his mid- to late seventies, he had a deeply tanned face, etched with wrinkles that reminded me of dried-up riverbeds. He had a small gray mustache and he wore a tan sport shirt and khaki slacks. He was a shade over six feet and seemed to be in remarkably good condition for a man his age.

"My name, Mr. Swann, is Karl Egeleise, but you know that, don't you? It is indeed a pleasure to make your acquaintance. It is a particular treat to have unexpected visitors."

"It didn't seem that way."

"I apologize. My people are very protective of me, sometimes erring on the side of caution." He spoke with a slight Germanic accent, but his words were clear and sharply enunciated.

"Usually one has only the opportunity to speak with Mexicans and Indians here," he continued. "The truth is, I sometimes find myself craving a civilized conversation with another Anglo. I don't mean that as any kind of slur, you understand. Just a fact. As you can see, I try to keep apace by reading as many international newspapers as possible. They are flown in each day. A luxury, I admit, but at my age a man in my position must be allowed such indulgences. I suppose a certain alienation from the affairs of the world is the small price I must pay for secluding myself in the mountains like this."

"I'd say you looked pretty comfortable here."

Egeleise smiled. "Have you had breakfast yet?"

"Yes."

"Some coffee perhaps." He moved to a large mahogany desk and pressed an intercom button. A moment later, the Indian appeared. "Juan, some coffee for Mr. Swann and myself." The Indian bowed and left.

I drifted over to the bookcase. Most of the titles were German editions. But I did spot one familiar title—*White African*, the book by Louis Leakey—and there seemed to be several art catalogues, many of pre-Columbian art exhibits.

Egeleise joined me. "I have little to do with my time now but read," he said. "My man tells me you speak Spanish."

"More like pigeon P.R. It gets me by, but just barely."

"It took me years to pick up English and Spanish."

"You seem to manage quite well."

"You're too kind, Mr. Swann."

"Take advantage of it while you can, Señor Egeleise," I said, mustering a bravado I did not have. The truth is, I felt totally vulnerable. I was way out of my element and he knew it as well as I did.

"I shall keep that in mind," he said.

Juan returned with a silver tray loaded with pastries and coffee.

"Thank you, Juan," Egeleise said, taking it from him.

We sat in chairs facing each other across a small table as we drank coffee. "Do you have many servants?" I asked, lifting my cup and blowing lightly across the coffee to cool it. The familiar smell helped calm me.

"Eight. I have not the need for that many, but it offers them a place to stay and something to do. They enjoy the life here. Few demands are made on them. This is a poor country, Mr. Swann, and any comfort, no matter how small, is welcome. Either my people live here with their families, or in the nearby village. They are a strange race. Descended from the ancient Aztecs who were quite an interesting breed of people. Did you know, for instance, that it is estimated that the Aztecs sacrificed approximately 250,000 humans each year? That, Mr. Swann, was out of a total population of nearly 25 million. About one percent. Amazing, isn't it? And what is even more amazing is that those sacrifices were devoured. The Aztecs, I'm afraid, for all their learning and intelligence, were cannibals."

Egeleise eyed me for a reaction. I suppose he thought I'd be shocked. Think again. I was born and raised in New York City. I had a wife who was killed in the kind of freak accident that most people wouldn't believe possible. I've "stolen" cars while their owners slept. I've found people who didn't want to be found. Nothing people do shocks me. It's what they don't do that sometimes throws me for a loop.

He continued. "Most people are surprised by this information because it's been largely covered up or ignored by most popular historians. It is an interesting sidelight, however, don't you think?"

He had a hardness about him that frightened me. This man was used to getting his own way and wasn't too worried about how he did it. I figured the best thing for me to do was listen and, in letting him talk, perhaps I could pick up some information that might help me, and then I'd get the hell out of there.

"We have evidence in the writings of Hernán Cortés, who conquered the Aztecs in 1521, and Bernal Díaz, who accompanied Cortés in this mission," Egeleise continued. "Here, allow me to read you something." He rose, went to the bookcase, and returned with a leather-bound book. "This is from Díaz's *The Conquest of New Spain*, a very enlightening tome. I came across it when I first moved to Mexico. He is speaking here about the town of Tlaxcala. 'We found wooden cages made of lattice-work in which men and women were imprisoned and fed until they were fat enough to be sacrificed and eaten. These prison cages existed throughout the country....'"

He stopped reading and looked up. "Fortunately, Mr. Swann, civilization has come a long way since. The sacrifices were carried out by priests and they took place atop the hundreds of steep-walled pyramids scattered throughout the Valley of Mexico. According to Díaz, the victims were taken to the pyramid tops where the priests," he began reading again, "'laid them down on their backs on some narrow stones of sacrifice and, cutting open their chests, drew out their palpitating hearts, which they offered to the idols before them. Then they kicked the bodies down the steps, and the Indian butchers who were waiting below cut off their arms and legs. Then they ate their flesh with a sauce of peppers and tomatoes.'"

"Very tasty."

"Not a pretty notion to men of our civilized nature, is it? But to the ancient Aztecs it was, in all probability, an extreme delicacy. I suppose it all depends upon your point of view."

"Point of view is one thing, eating people is another."

"We mustn't judge those from another time and another place, Mr. Swann. The skulls were then placed on a skull rack near each pyramid, alongside the skulls of previous victims. In Tenochtitlán, the royal city of the Aztecs and the precursor of Mexico City, Cortés' associates counted a minimum of 136,000 skulls on the rack. Díaz's accounts continue on to say that the Aztecs ate only the limbs of their victims, the torsos being fed to carnivores in zoos. It is also known that the Aztecs did not sacrifice their own people. Instead, they battled neighboring nations, using tactics that minimized deaths in battle and maximized the number of prisoners. You can, of course, see why."

"Nothing I admire more than a well-organized society."

Egeleise smiled. "An admiration we share."

"This is all very fascinating, an unexpected course in ancient hospitality, but..."

"Ah, but what is even more fascinating, Mr. Swann, is

a paper presented by an anthropologist named Dr. Michael Harner, who believes the Aztecs were cannibalistic not only for religious reasons, but also out of necessity. They ate humans in order to obtain protein in their diet. The ramifications are quite interesting, Mr. Swann. The Aztecs were forced to kill and devour their victims in order for them to continue to survive. Dr. Harner contends that a need for food, particularly during periods of famine, came to be a significant factor, especially as the human population of the Valley of Mexico grew to twenty-five million. In 1450, for instance, Aztec records indicated that famines were so severe that the royal granaries, which contained the grain surpluses of more than ten good years, were severely depleted."

"Like I said, Señor Egeleise, very interesting, but what's the point?"

He grinned. "Must there be a point, Mr. Swann? I simply found it immensely interesting in that, in a manner of speaking, this presents a very cogent argument for human sacrifices in order to maintain one's own existence, one's place in the world. I thought it might be helpful to familiarize a foreigner such as yourself with the rather strange, unconventional and sometimes bizarre ways of Mexico. Things are quite different down here, Mr. Swann. And I believe it is always advantageous to know where one is situated so that one may be cognizant of the proper form of behavior." He flashed a smile.

"In any case, Mr. Swann, I'm sorry if I sound pedantic. Certainly, a history lesson is not what you came here for."

"No, it isn't. The two names I passed on, they meant something to you, didn't they?"

"Did they?"

"If they didn't, then why did you let me in?"

He laughed and stroked his chin. "Maybe I'm just an old man with nothing better to do with his time. I could have sent you away, but I didn't. May I ask why you're in Acapulco?"

"I'm looking for someone."

"And who is it you're looking for? One of the two gentlemen you mentioned?"

"Jason Cheney, Harry Janus, they were the same person."

"How interesting. I wish I could help but, as I told you, those names mean nothing to me."

"Perhaps a photo might help." I showed him Janus's picture. He looked at it for a moment, a flicker of recognition appeared on his face, then he returned it to me. "Well?"

"It has a certain familiarity, mostly around the eyes, I think. I may well have seen this man before."

"And he didn't use the name Cheney or Janus?"

Egeleise flashed me an irritating enigmatic smile, then leaned back in his chair. "I didn't actually say I knew him, Mr. Swann. I merely said he looked familiar."

"You know, it's hot and I'm tired and I miss my own bed and a hundred other things, so do you think we could cut to the chase. Either I get your help or I don't. It's as simple as that. Just give me an answer and I'll be out of your hair."

"Allow me to change the subject for a moment. I promise I shall return to your lost man. What I'd like to know is what you have been told about me."

"Not much."

"Come now, Mr. Swann."

"Would it flatter you to hear you're known as a man who knows all and sees all?"

He laughed. "That depends upon whether it's a compliment or an insult. I'm afraid it is the nature of people, especially the Mexicans, who are a superstitious breed, to invent myths and legends. Jung did much work in this area, I believe. You're familiar with it, I'm sure. I'm afraid what with my eccentricities I have become one of those myths. Believe me, I have no extraordinary powers of perception, nor mysterious sources of knowledge. I keep to myself. It is rare that I leave these grounds. I have no need. Everything I want or need is here. You can see that. These superstitions amuse me. Allow me to tell you something about myself. The truth, if you will."

"That would be a refreshing change."

"I came from Germany during the final days of the war, thus there are rumors I was a Nazi fleeing the fall of Germany. Nonsense. I left because of the Nazis, not because I was one of them. I have no family. My wife died in the Berlin bombings. I never remarried. I am Swiss by nature, therefore neutral. War is an abomination. I prefer my music, my books and good art to politics. Hitler was the antithesis of all that and so I was, naturally, opposed to Hitler."

You and every other German, I thought.

"He disrupted my life and, quite frankly, I despised him for that. There came an opportunity to leave Germany and I took it. I was able to take some things of value with me, enough to make me comfortable in my new life. I went first to Argentina, but I'm afraid I found much the same atmosphere there—Perón, you understand—and so I came to Mexico where I found, shall we say, the social climate a bit more to my liking. I built this hacienda and began dealing in silver and other precious metals, which were quite plentiful here. I did quite well and found it unnecessary to ever work again, the dream of many, I might add. Occasionally, I find myself involved in business dealings, but that is rare and only as an amusement, a challenge, a diversion. You see, I have no need for additional funds. I would be less than honest if I did not admit that in Mexico I am considered a man of importance. *El Gran Alemán*, I'm called, a title which amuses me. People come to me for help and, in return, they give me information, most of which is useless, none of which I ask for."

"But you certainly don't discourage it, do you?"

"It is the nature of an important man that he keep informed and the Mexicans, at least those in this area, look up to me. They think of me as *un hombre muy importante*, so they present me with the information that keeps me in that position, a position they raised me to in the first place. People admire anyone with a little more knowledge than they themselves possess. Knowledge, Mr. Swann, can be a powerful weapon in the wrong hands. It is also, I might add, quite elusive. I am too old and far too complacent to put it to good use, but there is always the fear that I will. This is why I am still respected. Fear, you see, goes a very long way."

He sipped his coffee. I was going to say something but I decided against it. Silence is sometimes a great way to get information. People tend to abhor a vacuum and so they will fill it. Especially someone with an ego like Egeleise. He liked being in charge, he was used to it, and so it was better to let him think that he was.

"You've been very patient, Mr. Swann, and so now we shall come to the purpose of your visit. The man you are looking for, he was, shall we say, 'lost' some time ago, was he not?"

"That's a fair assumption."

Egeleise laughed. "You are a good poker player, Mr. Swann. You keep things close to your vest."

I simply smiled, keeping things as close to my vest as possible, even though I'd never actually owned one. The idea was to let him think that I was a lot more on top of things than I was.

"I believe we are well-matched. Each of us is armed with certain information that the other seeks. The unfortunate thing is that neither of us can be certain that the other is willing to part with the correct information, or all the information he possesses. If we were true antagonists, this would make for quite an interesting battle. But since we are not, it is of little consequence. The man you are looking for was here about a dozen years ago—in the late spring, if I'm not mistaken. He was a man of education and intelligence. He had a strong interest in the antiquities and also possessed a social conscience. He'd heard of me and sought me out. He knew I was an expert in pre-Columbian artifacts. We spent many hours together. I enjoyed his company. Originally he, too, was from Germany.

We had more than that accident of birth in common, however. We shared an interest in books, music, art and chess. He was a worthy opponent, I might add. He stayed with me for almost a month and then left. I'm afraid I never heard from him again."

Germany. Sally Janus had mentioned something about her husband being born in Europe. "What name did he go by?"

"William Doeppel."

"And where did he go from here?"

Egeleise smiled. "Ah, now we get to the heart of the matter, don't we. Without that information all else I've told you is worthless, is it not?"

"I guess it is."

"Well, I would like some information in return."

"I figured as much. You get nothing for nothing. It's just a matter of price now, isn't it?"

"It won't be expensive, believe me. It won't even come out of your own pocket. I'd simply like to know why you're looking for this man. And, Mr. Swann, I trust you'll tell me the truth."

"I have no reason not to," I said, but I knew if I told him everything I'd have nothing else to bargain with. I had to be very careful. Egeleise was no fool. I had to give him just enough, but not too much. "I've been hired by his wife to find him."

"Really?

"Yes. In New York, he was known as Harry Janus. He disappeared about a month ago. I'm trying to track him down. That's why I came to you." I figured that if I didn't admit that Janus was dead, Egeleise might tip his hand.

Egeleise didn't respond. Instead, he rose and moved to his desk. He picked up a pipe and pouch of tobacco and returned. He packed tobacco into his pipe, tamping it down rather violently as he spoke.

"I suppose it's my turn now. Your friend Janus, whom I knew as Doeppel, was a restless man. He was searching for something. People who search for something are usually searching for themselves. Sometimes, in order to give meaning to one's life, one immerses oneself in the lives of others. Thus the social conscience. An artificial device. A selfish not a selfless act. The man you're looking for, the man I knew as William Doeppel, disappeared into the hills almost a dozen years ago." He lit his pipe and puffed at it.

"I'm sure you have a few more details."

Egeleise puffed. "He traveled into the Sierra Madre del Sur mountains in the state of Guerrero."

"Why?"

"Perhaps to indulge his so-called social conscience," Egeleise said with a sneer.

"What have the Sierra Madres to do with a social conscience?"

"You have heard of Lucio Cabañas?"

"Afraid not."

"Cabañas is the leader of a band of rebels who have hidden themselves in the mountains for almost twenty years now. They are thought to be responsible for a long list of robberies, kidnappings and assassinations, all in the name of the 1910 uprising led by Emiliano Zapata. Their nucleus is a small band of perhaps thirty-five men, only five of whom are close to Cabañas. There are no known photographs of Cabañas with the exception of one which is, believe me, not him. There are no official birth records of the man, though officials in the towns of Atoyac and Chilpancingo have checked carefully. Cabañas is known as a master of disguise and has supposedly visited Acapulco quite frequently."

"What's this got to do with Doeppel?"

"What it comes down to, my friend, is whether there is, in fact, a man named Cabañas."

"I still don't see what you're getting at."

"Already your man has gone by three different names, why not a fourth?"

"You're suggesting Harry Janus, Jason Cheney and your William Doeppel were also Lucio Cabañas?"

"Precisely."

"That's not possible. The man I'm looking for has been in New York for at least six or seven years while your man Cabañas was supposedly terrorizing the countryside in the name of progressive revolution."

He smiled condescendingly. "Mr. Swann, stretch your imagination a bit. Allow me to present an example. In an automobile an electric charge is used to start the engine. Once the initial spark is set off, the engine continues to run itself with the use of petrol and the electric charge is no longer needed. Is that not so? I do believe it is not beyond the imagination to stretch this analogy to Señor Cabañas. My sources tell me that my old friend William Doeppel, when he disappeared into the hills years ago, became Lucio Cabañas. He remained Cabañas for some time, and once establishing this identity and setting this mini-revolution in motion, he disappeared as quickly and mysteriously as he arrived, leaving only the identity and legend of Lucio Cabañas to carry on. Whether or not he appointed a particular underling to this identity is not known to me, but is of little significance. The fact is, the man who was Lucio Cabañas is no longer in Mexico. Think about it, Mr. Swann. It would explain much, would it not?"

I'd been hired to find out who murdered Harry Janus and now, less than a week after I'd begun my investigation, it turned out I was looking for four different men, all of whom were the same man. I was beginning to have doubts as to whether any one of them actually existed. The more I looked, the more I found, the more confused I was. And so, instead of things getting clearer and the solution getting closer, I seemed to be drifting further and further away. And yet, as far as I could tell, I was following a clearly marked trail. Something was wrong.

"Mr. Swann, perhaps you would care for a drink. A brandy, perhaps?"

"Sure."

Egeleise rose, walked toward one of the bookcases, pressed a hidden button, and a bar miraculously appeared. He poured a snifter of brandy and returned.

"Aren't you having one?" I asked. "Not before noon, I'm afraid."

I took a sip. It went down very smoothly, though my throat began to burn a bit. "Why did you allow Doeppel to stay with you?"

"He interested me, much the way you do, Mr. Swann. He was different from me and yet, at the same time, we were quite similar. Frankly, I enjoyed his company. He was a fine conversationalist. We grew rather close."

"Close enough to keep track of him once he left."

"Only for a while. Once he left Mexico, he was lost to me. Outside this country, I'm afraid, is well beyond my scope of influence. I am neither omniscient nor omnipotent—despite what some would have you believe. This is why I'm interested in your search. This Janus, the man you believe to be Doeppel, what was he doing in New York?"

"Doing what everyone else in New York does, trying to keep his head above water."

"You'll forgive me, Mr. Swann, but I'm not quite sure what you mean."

"He was trying to get through life in one piece. As to the specifics, well, that's not up to me to say."

"Are you being purposely difficult?" he asked, a hint of menace in his voice.

"I'm sorry. It's just my nature. But the fact is, I have a responsibility to my client. If you want more information, you're going to have to ask her."

"I don't think that would be wise. Besides, it's only my curiosity I wish to oblige."

"I'd like to go where Doeppel went," I blurted out, though as soon as the words passed my lips I wondered what I was thinking. It had nothing to do with rational thought. I could just as easily get on the next plane and return to New York, tell Sally Janus what I'd learned about her husband, and call it a day. But I didn't. I'm not even sure why. Maybe it had to do with the way I'd skirted through life, never really committing to anything, always making sure that I had an escape route from the organized, responsible life that most people led. I was, I realized, a skip tracer in more ways than one. The truth was, I was always running away from my own life by trying to find others who ran away from theirs. Hopping off the bus before it reached its destination was what I did—to protect myself, maybe, from disappointment, from defeat. But now I had a chance to stay on for the entire ride, so that's what I was going to do.

"Could it be arranged?"

Egeleise frowned. Maybe I should have taken it as a sign, but I didn't. "In a country such as Mexico, anything can be arranged, but I would advise against it."

"Noted. But I'd still like to give it a go."

I hadn't even considered for a moment the consequences that might await me up there in the mountains. If I had, I'd sooner have walked into a blazing forest fire or, even worse, parts of the South Bronx after dark.

He shrugged. "Then I shall not attempt to talk you out of it. If that is what you want, I will give you Juan as a guide. I shall try to make contact with the rebels, but I cannot guarantee your safety. In the meantime, I will have Juan send back your driver. You will stay the night and leave early tomorrow." He rose. "Though I strongly advise against this action, I hope you are successful. As for now, my home is at your disposal." ⚲

# Montezuma's
## REVENGE

**B**EFORE BEING SENT TO MY ROOM for the night, I asked
to make one phone call. I told Egeleise I wanted to check
in with my family. I don't know why I lied, I just did.
Sometimes I do that, just to keep in practice. Lies are part of my
business—sometimes, you have to lie a little to get to the truth,
whatever the hell that is.

I was directed to the upstairs phone, where I was assured I'd
have privacy. I didn't believe him. I lied, why couldn't he? But
it didn't matter. I called Sally Janus. The first question out of her
mouth was, "Where are you?"

"Outside Acapulco."

"Enjoying yourself, I hope."

"Hardly."

"Well, I hate to mention this, Swann, but the meter is
running, even as we speak."

"Want to call it off ?"

"Not if you're making progress."

"I guess you could call it that."

"Tell me something."

"Your husband was down here, all right. For some time, as a matter of fact. I could tell more, but now is not the time. How do you feel about rock and roll?"

"I'm sure that's supposed to mean something, but for the life of me I can't figure out what."

"Ever hear of a group called 'Jason and the Argonauts?'"

"No. Why?

"They were very big."

"When, for God sakes?"

"Early eighties."

"I was listening to disco."

"Who wasn't? Ever hear of a song called, 'Stomp Out the Fires of My Heart?'"

"Could you hum a bar or two?"

"Very funny."

"Why are you asking?"

"I'll tell you when I see you. You know, to change the subject, I was sitting here thinking to myself, 'Swann, what are you doing here? Why are you in a strange country trying to piece together a man's life, a man you never even knew, a man that maybe no one ever really knew? Are you some kind of kinky biographer?' This is what I've been asking myself, because tomorrow morning I'm about to take a trip into the great unknown. I want some reassurance. I want to know why I'm here and not someplace else. Can you help me with this?"

She was silent. I tapped nervously on a table in front of me. Finally, she answered. "You're doing this because I'm paying you. I don't want you to get hurt, Swann, I really don't, but if you're as close as you think, then keep in mind the money. It's not an inconsiderable amount. There might even be a bonus in it for you."

Ah, money. The duck had descended and that was the secret

word. Looking around, I couldn't help but get a taste of what the secret word could buy. I was impressed, but the truth was, and I certainly wouldn't tell her this, I would have stayed on the case no matter what. Now, it was more than a matter of money; it was wanting to finish something I'd started, and it was wanting to put the world back in order by finding Harry Janus's killer. But that wasn't something I wanted her to know. Instead, let her think that I was motivated solely by cold, hard cash. That way, I could maintain the upper hand by letting her think that she controlled me.

"You are a very persuasive woman," I said.

"I know. Do you want me to wire you some more cash?"

"It would be helpful. I'm staying at the El Presidente in Acapulco."

"It will be there tomorrow."

"And so, I hope, will I."

JUST BEFORE 6:00 A.M. I AWOKE TO FIND JUAN, dressed in sandals, white cotton pants and an embroidered white cotton Indian shirt, hovering over me.

"Time," he said softly.

He moved silently to the window and drew open the curtains. Sunlight poured into the room, casting yellow puddles of light onto the floor and bottom half of the bed. I closed my eyes and rolled my head to the wall. Though normally a light sleeper, I hadn't heard him enter my room, nor did I hear him leave. I pushed the covers away and swung my legs to the floor. I stood there in the midst of one of the yellow circles, as if in a spotlight. For a moment, I was paralyzed as the light seemed to hold me in place. The bed beckoned me back. But I resisted.

In the bathroom, washing my face, I studied myself in the three-sided mirror. I tried to concentrate on one image, but couldn't. Every so often my glance wandered to one side and I caught sight of an eye—my own—staring back at me. I felt the growing stubble on my face, which made me look older. And yet there was something appealing about it. Camouflage. It made me feel like a different person, so I didn't bother to shave. I began to wonder how it would be to shed your skin and become another person whenever you liked. Evolving, evolving, evolving, into anything you wanted to be. Up from the Darwinian slime, crawling across mud banks, adding brain cell after brain cell. It seemed as if that's exactly what Janus was doing; with each new life he evolved into something more modern, less intuitive and more intellectual. But right now, the best I could do was to continue to let my beard grow.

Downstairs, Egeleise was seated at the large dining room table, set in front of a glass-encased cabinet containing numerous pre-Columbian figures.

"Good morning, Mr. Swann. You slept well, I trust." Groping for a chair, I sat down awkwardly.

"Your man is very light on his feet."

"A talent he picked up early in life. To live in the hills is to be a hunter and it is necessary for the hunter to be more stealthy than his prey, else he risks losing it."

I didn't much like Egeleise's habit of speaking in metaphors. Coming from him, everything sounded like a threat. He needn't have bothered. I could conjure up all the possible dangers. I yawned. "Sorry, I haven't slept much in the past few days."

"You don't have to make this trip, Mr. Swann."

"I know. Nice pieces," I said, gesturing toward the cabinet of figures behind me. "Pre-Columbian?"

"Yes, I became interested when I first arrived in Mexico. They say a man who collects things from the past does so because he is unsure of his own origins."

"I try not to meddle much in philosophical matters." I rapped on the table with my knuckles. "I'm more of a here and now kind of guy."

"No matter. Here, the collection of such art objects is not a difficult hobby to pursue. The hills are filled with unexpected treasures."

"I understand the government is clamping down on the appropriation of these treasures. Tired of having their national resources looted and sold for a fortune on the black market. Smuggling's big business nowadays, and evidently it's not only drugs. Isn't it illegal to own these kinds of objects?"

Egeleise tensed. "They are concerned, as well they should be. Antiquities are a national resource, as you say, and deserve to be protected as such. They tell a people where they've been and very likely where they are going. It is quite difficult now to get them out of the country. But, of course, I am in the country and have no intention of exporting them. And I obtained all these pieces well before any ban that you might be referring to."

"Of course."

I could hear music coming from another part of the house. I couldn't quite catch everything, but suddenly the refrain of "Stomp Out the Fires of My Heart" was repeated over and over again. It was Jason Cheney's song.

"Where's that coming from?" I asked.

"What?"

"That music."

He listened a moment. "The kitchen. I shall ask them to turn it down."

"It's all right. The song, do you recognize it?"

"I'm sorry, I wasn't listening. Should I have known it?"

"Have you ever heard of Jason and the Argonauts?"

"From mythology, of course."

"No. The rock group."

"I'm afraid contemporary music is not my forte."

I let it drop, but I wondered if Egeleise was taunting me. I stared at him to see if I could detect a hint in his face, but his expression remained unchanged. He relaxed and leaned back in his chair. "It is a long and arduous journey into the mountains, Mr. Swann. Best you begin early, before it becomes too hot to travel. The sun is unrelenting. The mountains are cooler, but the trip is not an easy one. Some breakfast, perhaps?"

"Please."

Moments later a heavy-set Indian woman appeared with a silver tray laden with coffee, eggs, toast and bacon. The familiar smells made me homesick. As I ate, every so often I'd look up to find Egeleise staring at me, and it unnerved me. I felt as if he was examining a specimen he was about to put under glass. It creeped me out. When my plate was empty, Egeleise rose and made a slow circle around the table. I found myself watching not him but his shadow, which, due to the peculiar way light passed through the enormous picture window, was far larger than the man himself. At one point in his stroll, his shadow fell on me, blocking out most of the light. He stopped a moment, then continued circling me.

"Your jeep is outside. Juan is waiting. You will go high into the mountains. A three-hour drive. The roads, I'm afraid, are not good. I have been fortunate enough to make contact with the appropriate people and you shall be allowed into the rebel camp. Certain precautions must be taken. However, they should not prove too inconvenient. You will remain safe as long as you heed Juan. He knows these men and the terrain and has been instructed to take care of you. Trust no one but him, for they will not trust you. I advise you to consider everything you hear very carefully. Remember, these men are very single-minded in their goals. And they are not beyond treachery."

"You mean they'd lie if it suited their purposes?"

"Yes."

"Just like the rest of us."

"If all goes well, Mr. Swann, you should return late this evening. I will see you then. *Auf wiedersehen.*"

∞

OUTSIDE, JUAN SAT ALONE IN THE JEEP. I walked toward him, my belly bulging from breakfast. I climbed in next to him. The back of the jeep was covered by a large green tarp. Provisions for the rebels, I assumed. Perhaps in payment for allowing my visit. At least that's what I told myself.

The Indian gunned the engine and we were off. Within minutes we were climbing into the mountains. The humidity that hung in the air for the last two days seemed to have vanished. The morning was cool and clear, the sun not yet having been up long enough to bake the air. A couple times I tried opening up conversation with the Indian, but each time he simply grunted and continued concentrating on his driving, which was, considering the circumstances, quite skillful. It wasn't long before I was filled with admiration for my Great Stone Faced Guide and Protector. Funny how close you can feel to people when you've got to depend on them.

We circled one mountain, then another, higher one. After nearly an hour, the road began to change. Now we were traveling up a dirt road just wide enough for one vehicle, and that one probably should have been a horse or mule. Dust, churned up by the wheels of the jeep, caught in my throat and eyes. I coughed and the Indian, without taking his eyes from the road or slowing down, reached into his pocket and handed me a bandana. He put his hand over his mouth, indicating where I ought to place it. I tied it, bandit-style, over my mouth and nose.

Soon the foliage became thicker and greener. We had suddenly slipped from one environment into another and, it seemed, from one time to another as well. At several points we lost the sun in the thick jungle overgrowth, and the Indian had to switch on the headlights as we traveled through a dark stretch.

Climbing steadily higher and higher, the air cooled, changing consistency, becoming thinner. I had to take deeper breaths in order to come up with the same amount of oxygen. Slowly, though, my lungs accustomed themselves to the change and I had an easier time of it.

Bouncing over bumps and loose rocks, I felt my stomach turn. The items under the tarp rattled about noisily. They weren't provisions. Too heavy for that. Guns, maybe. Or explosives. I tried to fight back the fear of having something explode behind me, sending me hurtling through the jungle.

The road ended. It had now been nearly three hours since we'd left the hacienda. The Indian pulled the jeep into a small clearing and stopped. He got out. I got out after him. Without a word, he began to walk.

"What about the things in the jeep?"

He ignored me and kept walking. I looked around. It was deathly quiet, except for the occasional chirping of a bird or the light rustling sound of a leaf caused by a slight breeze or the movement of a small animal. We were on the edge of a very heavy jungle area. Leave me in Bed-Stuy at midnight and I'm fine. I'll find my way home. But here, in the middle of a jungle, no way. And so I followed the Indian, who was already several yards deep into the underbrush.

Taking a machete from his side, the Indian wielded it expertly, chopping limbs surgically, clearing a well-defined path. I walked several steps behind. Every so often he looked around. I asked why. He didn't answer, but I got the distinct feeling we weren't alone.

After a half hour of chopping and slicing, the Indian stopped. I was beat. We'd been climbing uphill most of the way. My lungs burned and my legs ached. Though the temperature under the dense, dank overgrowth was probably still in the sixties, I was soaked with perspiration.

The Indian tucked his machete into his belt and studied a newly made slice taken from the side of a tree. He squatted, which I took as a sign that I was to do the same thing. Leaning against a tree, I wiped my face with the bandana, then slid down into a comfortable position. We sat there close to ten minutes, listening only to the sounds of the jungle. The smell of wet leaves nauseated me. Tiny bugs attacked my body, but I didn't have the strength to fight them off. Once, I started to say something, but the Indian put his finger to his lips, quieting me. We waited, for what I had no idea.

Ten minutes passed. I was getting edgy. I wondered if the Indian knew what he was doing. I wondered if I should have trusted Egeleise. I flirted with the notion of returning to the jeep and driving it all the way back to Acapulco.

I never heard so much as a twig break or a leaf rustle. They were on us that quick. The Indian, facing me, did not change his expression, though he must have seen them coming. He sat perfectly still, his arms folded across his chest, watching without emotion as someone stepped up behind me and wrapped a piece of cloth around my eyes. I jumped, then tensed. I tried speaking, but nothing came out. A woman's voice said, in English, to relax and that no harm would come to me.

Someone stood on either side of me, and I was helped to my feet. With a hand under each elbow, I was led forward. I couldn't be sure how many were with us now, because no words were exchanged. I didn't hear the sound of the machete, so I assumed the path we followed was one already broken.

The overgrowth was less thick. I felt the sun on my face, so I sensed I was being led east. Several times I lost my footing and stumbled, only to be caught and held upright by my seeing-eye dogs. Upward we walked, though not on a particularly steep incline and at a pace I could handle. Soon, we reached level ground and walking was easier.

We stopped. I heard voices. My blindfold was removed. We had arrived.

The rebel camp was a barren affair. Set under a grove of trees, it consisted of a few tents, a rundown wooden shack and the remains of a couple of small campfires. Scattered about the area were a half dozen bearded men wearing khaki Cuban-syle uniforms with cartridge belts slung across their chests.

I felt the men eye me warily. My heart started to speed up and my hands, at my sides, shrunk into fists. I turned and looked at the group who'd led me into the camp. There was one man, holding a rifle on me, the Indian, still expressionless, and a woman, dressed just like the men.

"My name is Diana Lopez," she said in perfect English. "Why did you come here?"

"I'm looking for Lucio Cabañas."

"Many look for Lucio, but those who have been successful now seek no one."

"I'm hoping I'll be the exception to the rule. I'm not here to make trouble. I'm hoping he can held me find a man I'm looking for."

"Lucio is not here."

"Where is he?"

"Doing the work of the revolution."

"Got any idea when he might be back?"

"You will have to talk to me."

I shrugged. "Okay, so how long have you been with Cabañas?"

"All my life," she said proudly. I noticed a rather startling resemblance to Sally Janus. Her coloring, the slim, wiriness of her body, the dark hair, the high cheekbones—they could have been cut from the same cloth.

"I have a photograph of the man I'm looking for. Is it all right if I take it out of my pocket?"

She nodded, then motioned to the man holding the carbine and he lowered the barrel until it pointed to the ground. I showed her the photo. Her body began to go limp, but she caught herself and straightened up. Her brow furrowed. I thought she was going to cry. She handed back the photo and said, "We will go inside and talk."

Inside the shack there was an old mattress on the floor, two cane chairs, a pot-bellied stove, several rifles leaning against the wall, boxes of ammunition on the floor, a few shelves filled with canned goods, stacks of old newspapers, and a heavy, wooden table. I sat in one of the chairs; she sat in the other.

"May I see the picture again, please?" she whispered.

I gave it to her. She held it close, in the darkness, and stared at it several moments.

"You know him, don't you?"

"Yes," she answered, her voice quivering.

"About a dozen years ago, wasn't it?"

"Yes."

"You knew him as Lucio Cabañas?"

She hesitated. "How do I know I can trust you?"

"I don't suppose you do. Do you trust Egeleise?"

"You are a friend of his?"

"No. I only met him yesterday."

"It's best not to trust men of such power. They have only their own interests at heart."

"I'm only using him to find out something about this man I'm looking for."

"Why are you looking for him?"

"This man...is dead. He was murdered...three weeks ago. I've been hired to find out who killed him."

She began to cry. I reached out and touched her shoulder, just something to let her know I was there. "He was Cabañas, wasn't he?"

"Yes," she sobbed, her shoulders heaving up and down.

"You knew his real name wasn't Cabañas, didn't you?"

"It was William Doeppel."

She began to calm down. I waited a moment then said, "Tell me about him."

She dried her face with her shirt sleeve.

"He came here twelve years ago," she began, her voice cracking. "There were not so many of us in the hills then. We heard of a gringo in the hills who was fighting for Mexico. I, along with others, came to join his cause." She began to sob gently again. I touched her again. She composed herself, then continued. "He worked hard. He organized. He was a student of history. Of warfare. A natural leader of men. He created the name Lucio Cabañas so that others would have one of their own to rally around. The legend followed. They sent hundreds into the hills after him, but Lucio was too clever. He was always one step ahead of them. Always he defeated them. He changed his appearance. He made them think he was somewhere he was not. After six months he left, leaving us only the name and the legend. To those close to him was left the task of making certain no one knew he'd gone. We were to see to it that all thought Cabañas was still in the hills leading the rebels, using many disguises. It was not difficult, señor. No one but I knew his real identity and no one outside the fifteen or twenty of us here knew what he really looked like. Now there are only two of us left. The others are dead, but they died with his secret."

"Does the name Cheney or Janus mean anything to you?"

"No."

"What do you know about Doeppel's past?"

"Nothing."

"You ought to know your friend Lucio was not what he pretended to be."

"He pretended to be nothing."

I saw the futility of telling her the truth, or my version of it, so I dropped it. "Who else knew Cabañas when he was here?"

"My brother, Carlos, the other who brought you here."

"What happened to the others?"

"Killed...disappeared." She shrugged. "Death calls us all, señor. Many things happen over twelve years time. After all, we are revolutionaries. We achieve our goals or become extinct, leaving our task to the next generation."

"Why did he leave?" I asked. She hesitated. "You can trust me. No one will know Cabañas is dead. I swear. Now, why did he leave?"

"He became involved in other matters."

"Like what?"

"Politics."

"What kind of politics?"

"I...I..."

"I need to know." I felt I was close, so close to an answer.

"Someone came into the hills and persuaded him to leave. I never saw or heard from him again. And now he's..." She began to cry again. While she cried I thought: Politics. What would a man who was dedicated to the violent overthrow of a government have to do with politics in the traditional sense?

"Who was this someone who came to get him? Egeleise?"

"No."

"Is there anything else you can tell me?"

"If you want to know more, why not speak to your friend, Egeleise. He is the man who knows everything, is he not?"

Suddenly, there was a commotion outside.

"What's that?"

"Sshh," said the girl, holding her hand over my mouth. She moved to the window, making sure she wouldn't be seen from outside. I could hear the Indian's voice amongst the others, but I couldn't understand what was being said.

Suddenly, the girl grabbed my arm and pulled me toward the back of the shack. "You must leave. Quickly, or they will kill you."

"Why?"

"If you do not leave now, you will not live. The Indian wants you dead. We will be blamed."

"What?"

"Please," she said, pushing me toward a back window. "You must—"

"Okay, okay, but tell me, what's going on?"

"The jeep that brought you carried weapons from Egeleise."

"For what?"

"Artifacts. Drugs."

I started to ask what more she knew, but I heard movement coming our way. She pushed me more firmly.

"Wait. You know more about Cabañas's leaving."

"I know only that the man who came for him was Alemán. Lucio called him the man 'from the four power city.' His real name was Horst. Lucio knew him from before. He..." There was more noise from outside, voices, clicking sounds that I took to come from the cocking of rifles. "You must go now," she said with more urgency.

I knew I was in trouble and had no intention of ending my life there in the mountains. "I don't know how to get out of here. How am I going to get back?"

"Run to the trees. If you go west you will find the trail that brought you here. Look for the mark on the tree in the clearing where you waited. Follow the trail back to the jeep. It is still there. Hurry!" She pushed me toward the open window. Outside the voices were more heated, louder. I started to panic, making my way toward the window to escape.

"Remember," the woman said, pointing toward the jungle. "Follow the path."

"Egeleise is behind this, isn't he?" I asked, one foot dangling over the window sill.

"He is a man interested only in money and power. Lucio was a threat to him. They were friends who became enemies. For many years he has searched for him. Perhaps he suspects you can lead him to Lucio. If Egeleise cannot have the answer to where Lucio is, he will destroy you to preserve his power. You must go!"

"What about you?"

"My people will protect me."

I slid out the window and ran, stumbling, toward the safety of the jungle. When I reached the tree line I looked back in time to see the Indian wielding his machete with the same grace and skill he'd used to clear the jungle path. Only this time he was using it on one of the rebels. Carlos. The rebel, a shrill sound emanating from deep within him, fell as the machete tore open his belly. I could see the blood spurt, spraying the earth red. I thought of Egeleise's tales of the ancient Aztec's and their inhuman sacrifices. I thought of some lethal gene passed down through scores of ancestors until it settled in the Indian. I thought of going back to help, but I knew I couldn't. I had no weapon. I would be no match for the Indian and his machete.

Another quick slash sliced Carlos's throat. There was silence. I glanced at my hands and saw they were shaking. I tried to move, but my feet seemed planted in cement. I looked back toward the shack and saw that several of the other rebels had taken the Indian's side and were attacking their comrades. I knew if I stayed I'd be next. They'd come and find me. My only chance was to get a head start and hope those loyal to Diana and her brother would win out. Again, I tried to move and this time my feet seemed to respond. I began to run, searching for the trail that would lead me back to safety—away from this murder and madness.

As I ran, I heard the air-piercing sound of a woman's death scream echoing through the otherwise silent jungle. I stopped, but it was too late. There was only enough time to save myself and break with yet another link to Harry Janus's past. ⚡

# A Close
# SHAVE

I RAN DEEPER INTO THE JUNGLE, losing all sense of direction. I ran desperately, wanting only to get as far away as possible. The farther I ran the more lost I became. Thorns from dangling vines stung my face and body. Branches snapped at me, raising large, ugly crimson welts. But I felt nothing and ran on as though running would purge the fear I felt, as if it would lift me to another time, another place. I ran with those blood-curdling shrieks of death tearing at me, vibrating inside me until they threatened to split me in half. Not even the sound of my footsteps, of my heart beating faster, pounding louder inside my chest until the sound seemed to reach outside me, not even that could erase the terrible image of the Indian's sharp, slashing arm.

Finally, I had to stop. My hands over my ears, I leaned, panting, against a tree.

My shirt and plants were plastered to my body by my own

perspiration. Only then did I realize how lost I'd become.

I listened. Hearing nothing other than the squawking of birds I couldn't see and the buzzing of insects that seemed to follow me down the mountain, I grew calmer. My breathing became more regular. I thought if I headed west I could pick up the path. By moving quickly, I might even be able to beat the Indian back to the jeep.

Breaking through tiny openings in the dense foliage, the sun cast small discs of light onto the moist ground and created a path for me to follow. I imagined my own death: alone in the jungle, body rotting, eaten by maggots, becoming a part of the earth, far away from the concrete jungle in which I grew up, and even farther from El Barrio where I'd spent my time since the death of my wife, where I was destined to end my life. I didn't want to die alone and in a place so unfamiliar. But where did I want to die? Where wouldn't I be alone?

Though my throat burned and my legs felt heavy, I kept on, craving something familiar, something that I could connect to the rest of my life.

I found what looked to be the right path. It was no wider than the center aisle of a New York City bus, yet it looked enormous to me. I listened and heard nothing. I wondered if the Indian knew a shortcut and would be waiting for me ahead. I started down the path, moving slowly and quietly. If the Indian was behind me, I wouldn't hear him and he would be on me without warning. One quick slash with his glinting blade and I'd be in two neat, equal pieces. It was this chilling thought that kept me going.

I lost patience with this slow pace and began to jog downhill. Eventually, I found myself getting a runner's high. My weariness seemed to fade and I was on automatic pilot. The memory of the screaming seemed far behind me, and now I heard only the sound of my own footsteps crushing damp leaves and breaking twigs. I ducked and swerved to avoid branches and often changed direction in order to follow the winding trail. Soon,

I came across the small clearing where we'd rested, found the slices taken from the tree, and located the Indian's trail that led back to the jeep. Just before reaching the spot where I thought we'd parked the jeep, I picked up a heavy stick for protection and stopped to listen for any unusual sounds.

Nothing. I stepped forward, until the jeep was in plain sight. I moved stealthily toward it, and when I reached it, I bent over and looked to see if the key was in the ignition. It wasn't there. For a moment, I panicked, but then I remembered that I didn't need a key. And, for the first time in days, I was back in my element: hotwiring cars. After fiddling with a few wires, I heard the welcome sound of the motor turning over. I revved it up until the roar filled the still air. I shouted at the top of my lungs, then gunned the engine and was off.

I rode a mile or so, then stopped. I picked up the tarp. In place of rifles, I found two canvas satchels. Inside, there were several sealed plastic bags filled with a brown, powdery substance. Heroin. There were also another few bags filled with a white powder. Cocaine. Not a bad return for a jeep load of weapons, I thought as I zipped up the bags, replaced the tarp, and started off again.

Getting down the mountains was easy. Though I'd paid little attention to the route up, I simply followed the dirt road down until I came to the paved one. Finally, the air became stickier and, looking back, I saw the mountains looming behind me. By the time I was within sight of Egeleise's hacienda, it was dusk. My stomach tightened as I pressed down on the accelerator and sped by.

Reaching the outskirts of the beach area, I abandoned the jeep in the sand and wiped my fingerprints off anything I touched. I left the two satchels of drugs in the jeep, figuring after I reached the hotel, I'd anonymously let the cops know about it, and they could trace the jeep back to Egeleise. That should cause him at least a few problems, though it might be no more than greasing a few of the right palms to have the whole incident buried in Mexican sand. ✦

# Adiós Pancho,
## EMELIANO
## AND VICTORIANO

I ADDED IT ALL UP. Consider first that Harry Janus had originated in Deutschland; less than a week before his death he'd received a call from Berlin from a mystery man named Horst; according to Diana Lopez, the name of the kraut who came up into the hills and dragged Cabañas away from his own private revolution launched in honor of Zapata was named Horst, and from Berlin, no less. So now I'd just follow the Yellow Brick Road to Berlin. There I'd get in touch with Kurt Weill, Sally Bowles and company. And I'd find Horst. And maybe the reason for Janus's murder. And maybe his killer. And maybe who Harry Janus really was. Pass Go and collect two hundred dollars. It was merely a matter of time and perseverance.

The next morning, after a fitful sleep, I stared sleepily at myself in the bathroom mirror. I hadn't shaved in four days and the growing brown and gray stubble was beginning to chafe. I massaged my rough cheeks and decided against the blade. I looked like Robert Mitchum after a bad night. From the corner of my eye, I caught the glistening chrome frame of the mirror above the sink, and I had a quick image of the Indian, his machete gleaming in the sunlight. That decided the matter once and for all. My razor slipped into the sink. The hollow clinking sound it made on the porcelain startled me.

Staring into the mirror again, I imagined myself with a full beard. I went back to the room, opened up my satchel, and pulled out the photo of Janus. I returned to the bathroom and held it up to the mirror. There was a definite resemblance. I laughed it off, but somehow it didn't seem at all funny.

I examined the photo closely. Long crease lines ran through various portions, dissecting Janus's body in several places, giving it a jigsaw puzzle effect. It looked as if it could have been taken just after Cabañas came down from the hills. Adding yet another dividing line through the body, I folded it and shoved it back in my pocket.

I checked out of the hotel, forking over a wad of Mexican play money. Parked directly in front of the hotel was the battered Ford, driven by my good amigo and former tour guide, José, who, in his favorite position in the front seat, dozed behind the wheel. Moving closer, I noticed a large fly buzzing noisily against the windshield. It bounced against the dashboard several times, then exited out the window. All the while José remained blissfully in dreamland.

The roof of the car, a giant reflector, shot beams of bright sunlight into my eyes. I reached for my sunglasses and stood by the side window, but José did not stir. I rapped on the car roof with my knuckles. He awoke with a start, pushing his straw hat back on his head.

"Remember me?" I asked, leaning my face into the open window.

"Si, señor, I am glad to see you. I was worried for you. I did not like leaving you up there alone with Señor Egeleise. When the señor's hombre came out to deliver the dinero along with your message, I asked to see you, but he would not allow it. Many men have gone up there and some have not returned."

"Nice time to tell me that, José."

"Your face...."

I touched my cheek. "Ran into a few low-flying branches. I need a ride to the airport. You up to it?"

"Certainly, señor."

I slid into the back seat. A familiar stench of rotting food was in the air, the same sort of smell that had been in the hotel where Janus had been murdered. I smiled. No matter where I was, I seemed to be in the same place. Events all seemed to tie into each other, but I still needed that one missing piece of information that would make all the rest come together.

As the cab pulled off, I found myself watching several large horseflies as they buzzed around a small chunk of food on the floor. I watched, nearly hypnotized, as they circled the food, dove into it, tearing small hunks off, then bouncing off only to return a few seconds later to repeat the scavenging process, further disembodying the rapidly vanishing morsel.

"Señor," José said, as we pulled into the airport. "I am sorry your stay in Acapulco was so short and unpleasant. It is my sincere wish that you found what you were looking for?"

"Not quite."

"Perhaps you leave Acapulco too soon."

"Not soon enough. The man I'm looking for was here, but he isn't anymore. How much?"

"Fifty pesos." I was in a generous mood, perhaps because I was leaving Mexico. I gave him most of what I had, which amounted to almost 100 pesos. "*Muchas gracias*, señor. You are a very generous man."

"*De nada*," I said, as I opened the cab door and got out.

The fresh warm air filled my lungs, quickly replacing the foul, sour odor of the cab. As I looked back I saw José, his Ford pulled up in line behind several other cabs, tip his straw hat forward over his eyes and lean back against the front seat to wait for the next bunch of gringo touristas. Half an hour later I was in the air again, headed back to L.A. ⚹

# The Red
## SCARE

BACK IN L.A. NO BANDS PLAYED, no flags waved, no bouquets were tossed at me, so I slipped back into town as unobtrusively as when I'd first arrived from the east. Paranoia now had a steel-fisted grip on me. I kept looking over my shoulder for the copper-faced Indian, and now, ahead of me, I kept an eye peeled for the Mutt-and-Jeff team of hoods. I moved through the crowds on the balls of my feet, like a boxer, hunched over, body tense, ready for action, my arms poised in front of me. I was set for any unexpected attack, thus making no attack unexpected.

Once inside the terminal, I headed straight for the Lufthansa desk and purchased a ticket to Berlin. I forked over my credit card. The gorgeous blonde ticket agent, with hard angular Teutonic features, punched the little gadget with all the buttons and lights on it, and a red bulb flashed on and off menacingly.

My pulse quickened, my hands began to perspire. Everything I'd ever done wrong in my life, real or imagined, became magnified. Those unpaid parking tickets. Those years I never bothered to file my income tax. Tearing tags off mattresses. On the outside, though, I was as cool as the other side of the pillow. "Something wrong?" I asked.

"It is just the machine, sir," she said in her strongest, most competent German voice as she took complete command of the situation.

"We have been having some trouble with it today. It's nothing. I'll try again."

You do that, *fraulein*, I thought, leaning up against the counter as I strained forward to get a little better look at her legs. Slim, long, tanned, muscular in all the right places. Aryan legs. Legs leading to something even better. If this was a preview of what I'd find in Alemánia, then I was certainly going to like it...if I ever got there.

The next time the girl pushed the buttons, the light came up green and all was well. Just a slight screw-up. The German Lorelei smiled, flashing thirty-two straight, white, rank and file Aryan teeth, handed back my card with a hand that was soft and well-manicured, and then followed up with my validated ticket. It was not a hand used to punching keys, I thought, making sure to touch her fingers as I accepted my ticket. A tingling sensation traveled through my arms and downward, and I wanted to ask if she had any plans to visit the Fatherland real soon. But the guy waiting behind me nudged his bag into the back of my knees, so I had to move on.

I had an hour and a half to kill before the plane took off. I thought I'd better check with the hotel before leaving, to see if there were any messages. I donned my movie-star shades and found a phone and dialed the Sheraton.

"Yes, Mr. Swann, Sally Janus would like you to call her as soon as possible."

I hung up, then dropped another coin into the slot. I dialed Sally Janus, reversing the charges. It was late back in New York, so it took a while for her to answer. When she did, her voice sounded groggy.

"Where are you?" she asked.

"LAX."

"Are you coming home?"

"Not exactly."

"Well, exactly what *are* you doing?"

"Checking your finances again."

"What's that supposed to mean?"

"It means I was wondering how committed you are to finding your husband's killer."

She hesitated a moment. "Very."

"You don't sound sure."

"Look, I'm not paying you to question my integrity," she said, her tone suddenly changing to stern. "I loved my husband."

"I'm sure you did. I just want to know how committed you are to finding his killer. And why is it so important to you?"

"Because I need closure, that's why."

"Then how would you feel about springing for a ticket to Berlin and a couple day's expenses over there?"

"Swann, you wouldn't be holding me up, would you?"

"If you don't trust me, you can call it quits right now," I bluffed, seeing as I already had one foot on the plane.

"Tell me what you have so far."

I didn't want to get into details. I'm not sure why, but, just from picking up something from the tone of Sally Janus's voice, I was beginning to doubt that she even cared who killed her husband. But then, why would she have hired me? There was something wrong here, but I just couldn't put my finger on it.

"I found that he had at least two other identities before you knew him. A Mexican revolutionary named Lucio Cabañas and a German named William Doeppel."

"Oh, please."

"You think I'm making this stuff up?"

"I don't know. It is pretty fantastic. Why Germany?"

"Because I think the answer we're looking for is there."

"All right. Two days. That's it. If you don't find anything by then I'll have to pull the plug."

"Okay. Two days. That's all I'll need. Did your husband ever talk about Germany?"

She was silent a moment. "Not that I can remember."

"Then what made you think he was originally from there?"

"I don't know. Maybe we were watching a movie and he pointed out a place in Germany that he recognized. I can't think of any other way."

"What about someone named Horst?"

"Horst who?"

"Would it make a difference?"

"No."

"Okay, go back to sleep. I'll be in touch."

I hung up, dropped in another coin, and dialed the Sharp house, just to see if I stir up a little trouble. Carole Cheney answered. "Yeah?" she answered gruffly.

"It's Swann."

"Oh, lover, you sound different," she purred. "Where are you?"

"Never mind. Is your husband home?"

"'Fraid not. Jackie's never home anymore. Do you think maybe he's found someone else? Why don't you come over here and keep me company, lover? I could sure use company. I'm gettin' kinda tired of playin' with that damn dog."

"I want you to give him a message."

"I'm not very good at messages, lover. I get them all screwed up. Why don't you come over here and give it to him yourself?"

"I'd like to, but I've got one foot out the door. Listen, your hubby the jealous type?"

"What's Jack's is Jack's, if you know what I mean. You worried about our little...tête-à-tête?"

"Not in the least."

"Then what's the problem?"

"No problem. Just tell him I ran into a friend of his down in

Mexico. A German fellow named Karl."

"What's that supposed to mean?"

"Be nice to him and maybe he'll clue you in. Gotta go."

Cheney seemed awful anxious to get me over there. If there was a connection between Egeleise and Sharp, as I suspected there might be, then Egeleise might have gotten in touch with Jackie-baby. I suspected there might be some fireworks around the Sharp household that evening. Too bad I wouldn't be around to catch them. ⚔

# BERLIN

*Acapulco, Mexico to Los Angeles to Berlin*

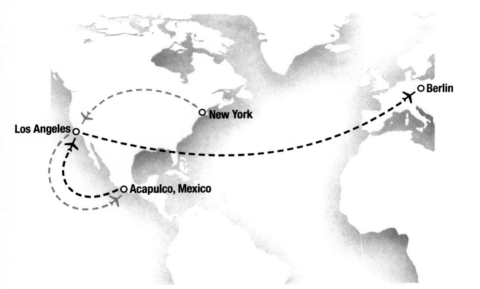

# You Haf Relatives
## IN GERMANY?

A S I STOOD ON THE CUSTOMS LINE, holding a nearly empty suitcase, declaring nothing, my mind raced several moves ahead. Once settled in Berlin, I'd try to pick up Janus's trail by checking out the several names I'd brought with me. If I was lucky, I might even get a lead on the mysterious Horst.

If I thought I was out of my element in L.A. and then in Mexico, here I was really an alien from another planet. There were uniformed police throughout the terminal and, perched precariously on the edge of a chaotic world that seemed to be inhabited by nightmarish monsters wreaking all kinds of havoc, these symbols of order and discipline which should have put me at ease did just the opposite. Here in the Old World, especially

Germany, uniforms historically symbolized something other than the security I was looking for, and this authoritarian ambiance made me even jumpier. Who knew how many smiling, bulbous-nosed, fleshy, red- cheeked faces hid Nazi mentalities?

Before my nerves had the chance to get shakier, I found myself standing bareheaded at the curb with a light but unrelenting rain assaulting me and blurring my vision through my dark glasses. Beads of water skidded down the dark green lenses, leaving long vertical streaks and giving me a bad case of double vision. I stood there a moment, lost in thought, until a Mercedes cab screeched to a halt in front of me, spraying water on my shoes and the bottoms of my pants. Shaking my legs free of water, I got in and told the driver to take me to the Hilton, which I chose from an airport travel folder for its proximity to the Hall of Records I thought I needed in my search. Located in the post-war center of Charlottenburg, it was a good jumping off point. Riding through the rain-slick streets, my cab passed within sight of the new Kaiser Wilhelm Memorial Church, rebuilt next to the remains of the original cathedral which had been pounded into oblivion by giant B-17s while A. Hitler crouched low in his cozy little bunker hideaway, paralleling the sewer system of the city. There, with his Bavarian peasant tootsie, Little Eva, they drank steins of beer and nibbled on finger sandwiches and desserted on extraordinarily flaky Napoleons. Inside the church stood a white marble figure of Christ, arms blown to smithereens by Allied bombing raids.

I checked into the hotel and went up to my room on the 23rd floor. Immediately, I was aware of the similarity between this room and the last two I'd been in. It could have been the same furniture—nondescript, dark brown wood—and an armoire that held a television and several drawers to keep my clothes in. Even the flowered bedspread looked the same as the ones in my rooms in Acapulco and L.A. In the past five days I'd been in three different hotel rooms in three different cities and yet it was as if I hadn't moved an inch.

I went to the window, drew back the curtain and looked out over the Tiergarten, the second largest zoo in the world, also housing the world's largest aquarium. The rain was falling harder now and the zoo was pretty much deserted, both animals and captors having retreated to shelter. The only signs of life were cars skidding by over slick, rainy streets, their headlights reflecting skyward. The window was sealed shut, so I was locked in, protected by a large sheet of glass that reflected my own image back at me. I looked past myself, out onto the city. To the east, a giant phallus stabbed into the dense gray air—the bronze Victory Column commemorating German triumph in the Franco-Prussian War. Further on, in the same direction, the sky turned even darker, almost charcoal in color. Here the large buildings ended abruptly and, according to my guidebook, it was at this point that a long, winding wall had once cut the city in two, reminding people that the east and west didn't always shake hands. Gazing past the column into the dark gray, low-hanging clouds, I couldn't help but think of John le Carré spy novels, like *The Spy Who Came In From the Cold*, which told of treachery, deceit and danger, often from within, all of which intermingled freely with my own personal intrigue.

I've never been a particularly religious man. But what I do believe in is the concept of an ordered world that gives a certain meaning to life. Ultimately, there is a logic. It may be twisted, but it's there. I was committed to the idea that everything ultimately makes sense, that from chaos comes order. When I finally reached the end of the line, when I finally found this character Horst, everything would fall right into place. And it was this knowledge that spurred me on, that made me anxious to get started.

I awoke from a short nap, and all the telltale signs of a cold were there: sneezing, headache, all-around stuffiness. I felt weak and listless, as though in a few short hours, energy had been almost completely drained from my body. My head was a little fuzzy, and I felt I was thinking and moving in slow motion.

By the time I left for the Hall of Records, the rain had stopped; but the day remained ominous, as dark gray clouds still hung threateningly over the city. It was now early afternoon and more people were out on the streets. Inside the government building, I managed to find someone who spoke passable English, a young clerk who directed me to a large room filled with books that housed the city's birth records. The high-ceilinged room, filled with the heavy odor of stale air, was quiet and nearly empty. I located the section where the proper ledgers were stored and, with a newly purchased box of tissues beside me, I set to the tedious job of wading through each book that contained a record of births for a period of five years. Seated at a long wooden table, I began with the one marked 1950-55. Working backwards, I checked the ledger for the names Janus, Jenner, Cheney and Doeppel. Halfway through my box of tissues, I made a connection. In 1951, a child named Wilhelm was born to Werner and Karla Doeppel. Excitedly, I copied out the entry.

After replacing the ledger, I found a phone booth and directory. I looked up the name Doeppel, finding two, neither of them Wilhelm, Werner or Karla. I copied them down, dropped a coin into the slot and dialed the first number. I got a woman who spoke only German. Unable to communicate, I gave up, figuring I'd have to visit to the addresses to get what I needed.

The first was in the Wedding district of Berlin. Arriving by cab, I found the six-story flat, punched the buzzer under the nameplate marked Doeppel, 3B, and stepped back. A moment later I was buzzed into the building. I walked up two flights and knocked on the door.

"*Wer es ist?*" a man's voice asked.

I didn't quite know what he was asking, but I figured saying, "I'm an American. My name is Henry Swann. I've come to ask you a few questions about someone you may have known after the War," might do the trick.

"Wait," the voice answered in English. There was a shuffling sound, the closing of a door, and then the familiar sound of a lock unlatching. The door opened. "Come in," the voice ordered.

The occupant was an old man, in his mid-seventies. He was tall, though bent and thin with white hair. He walked slowly into a poorly lit room and I followed. "Sit down, please," he said, pointing to an old, threadbare couch that gave off a musty odor. The old man seemed remarkably calm, almost as if he'd expected a visitor.

"Coffee?" the old man asked.

"No, thanks," I said, looking around the room. There were two windows with the draperies drawn. There was a fireplace and a few primitive paintings of country scenes hanging on the walls. There was a closed door at the other end of the room. I thought I heard a sound and wondered if there was someone else in the apartment. "Your English is quite good," I said.

"Thank you."

"Where did you learn?"

"I was a teacher of English," the old man said, lowering himself gently into a chair facing me.

"I'm sorry to intrude. I won't keep you long. I'm looking for someone named Wilhelm Doeppel."

The old man remained motionless. His eyes, bright blue, were riveted to a point somewhere in the middle of my chest, pinning me to the spot. There was something very familiar about those eyes.

"I am afraid you have made a mistake. My name if Joséf, not Wilhelm. You have come to the wrong address. I am sorry."

"Perhaps you know of him then. Or perhaps you know of Werner or Karla Doeppel."

The old man crossed his legs while I tried to find a comfortable position for my hands. I stared at the door at the other end of the room, listening for sounds coming from behind it, but hearing nothing.

Finally, the old man spoke. "Why are you looking for these people?"

"It's Wilhelm I'm looking for. I'm working for his wife. In America. Do you know any of these people?"

The old man exhaled slowly as he uncrossed his legs. His hands, gnarled and liver-spotted, covered his knees. I noticed a vein pulsating wildly in his neck. It was his only movement now—the only visible sign of life other than his voice, which seemed to be piped in from somewhere outside him. Strong and even, the movement in his neck did not seem to be in sync with his frail body.

"No," he said.

"Relatives, maybe?"

He remained silent; only his vein moved.

"I'm not here to make trouble. I only want to find Wilhelm Doeppel."

The old man lifted his eyes to mine, though he looked as if he was looking straight through me. He took a breath. "Sometimes a man who loses himself does not want to be found. From my own generation there are many who do not want to be found. They scattered themselves around the world. The reasons are self-evident."

"This is a man who has to be found."

The old man cracked a smile. "A matter of life and death?"

"You could say that."

The old man sighed. He sucked in another breath and said, "Werner was my brother. He is dead now. His wife, Karla, and the child, Wilhelm, disappeared soon after his death. I know nothing of their whereabouts. I am afraid that you have come a long way for nothing."

"How and when did he die?"

"What does it matter?"

"I won't know till you tell me."

"A car accident. In 1962."

"Do you know a man named, Horst? I think he was connected in some way to Wilhelm."

The old man laughed. The laugh turned into a violent

cough. Clutching his throat, he gagged twice. I thought I was going to lose him right there, but he came back. "You, Herr Swann, you have heard of an American named John?"

I got the point. "This was someone who knew Wilhelm. Someone from his past. Maybe you can help me find him."

The old man ran his hands through his disheveled hair. His body relaxed. The vein in his neck slowed. He cleared his throat and said, "There was a Horst. He was a friend of Wilhelm's when they were small. He was a neighborhood child. Wilhelm disappeared when he was about twelve. Horst was a bit older, perhaps."

"What was his last name?"

"Kleiner."

"Where is he now?"

"In Berlin. In the old East."

"Do you know exactly where he's living? Anything that might help me find him? What he does for a living, maybe?"

"I am afraid that Kleiner is no longer the same Kleiner he was thirty years ago. His name is now Martel. Charles Martel. He changed it when he joined the Communist party. Beyond that, I can tell you nothing."

Good enough, I thought. Now the trail seemed to be leading someplace really important, and I was beginning to feel I was close to a breakthrough. Kleiner. Martel. Janus. Doeppel. Jenner. Egeleise. And all the other names finally seemed to be creating a pattern.

"I appreciate what you've told me," I said.

"I have told you nothing that you would not have found out eventually for yourself. I have only shortened the time for you. Martel will not help you in your search. Do not look for him. Even if you found him, he would not help you. I am afraid I will have to excuse myself now. I am an old man. My heart is not so good. I must rest."

"I understand. But aren't you curious about your family? After all, Wilhelm is your nephew."

"Everyone in my family is dead now. Wilhelm has been gone for thirty years. After so many years, a man does not need a long lost relative. I am happy to leave well enough alone. Perhaps, Herr Swann, you should do the same. Goodbye, now."

The old man got up and moved toward what I assumed was the bedroom. He opened the door just wide enough for him to squeeze through, leaving me alone in the room.

Queer, I thought, leaving me alone like that. I remained still for a few seconds, waiting for someone to emerge from behind the closed door. It was odd the way he left me there, and I strained my ears to hear the muffled noises coming from behind the heavy oak door. But nothing happened, so I got up and made my way toward the door. After all, I'd gotten what I'd come for: I'd made the connection between Doeppel and Horst. ⚹

# Ich Bin
# EIN BERLINER

IMADE MY WAY BACK TO THE HOTEL trying to make sense out of the information I'd obtained from Joséf Doeppel. There were so many new pieces of the puzzle, and I knew I needed help to sort them out. I had no idea about the intricacies of the spy business and I was pretty murky when it came to World War II and Cold War history.

I needed a refresher course, so I called Jeff Weber, a fellow I knew back in New York who I thought might be able to help me out. When I first met him, he was fresh out of the military, a real gung-ho guy. The first one out of the trenches. The one with his hand over his heart when the national anthem is played at ballgames. The last I'd heard, he was in government service—supposedly working for the USIA, which I always thought was just a euphemism for cloak and dagger stuff. Jeff was just the type to go into CIA work, but of course he never owned up to anything like that. In any case, we'd swap favors every once in a while—if I needed information on someone, I'd go to him and somehow, I didn't ask how, he always came up with a contact who could help me. In return, I'd toss him tickets to Yankees or Knicks games that I got from bail bondsmen I worked with. I knew he had contacts, and if I approached him the right way, he'd probably want to show off by helping me. I was right.

"So what's this all about, Swann? And where the hell are you?"

"I'm in Germany and I've got this investigation going."

"Investigation? Germany? The last I heard, you were busy staking out cars in the South Bronx."

"Well, things have changed."

"For the better, I hope."

"Well, that depends. I need to talk to someone who can give me some information about the intelligence business during the Cold War."

"Jesus, that's ancient history, pal. Didn't you hear that the Red Menace is over?"

"You know someone who can help me or not?"

"Well, yeah, I guess. You might try Stan Powers. He works out of the Embassy in Berlin. Give him a call. Tell him I told him to help you, that you can be trusted with secrets. You can be trusted, can't you, Swann?"

"Trust is my middle name."

"Yeah, well then, where's that twenty bucks you owe me from the last Knicks game we went to?"

"It's in the mail, Jeff. Promise."

"Yeah, I'm sure."

I called Stan Powers. I gave him Jeff's message. He hesitated a moment, and then said, "Call back in half an hour and I'll try to have something for you."

I didn't feel like waiting in my room, so I went across the street and took a table facing the sidewalk in a small outdoor café. It was nearly four o'clock and the weather was just breaking. Small patches of blue were popping up above the city. The wind, blowing in from the west, molded the clouds and connected the emerging pieces of the sky, forming larger areas of bright blue, and producing sunlight, which poured through the broken cloud cover and dried the streets. The city began to take on a new face. The grayness of the morning gave way to a more Technicolor pallete.

After a couple of minutes the waiter, fat and smiling, an Aryan Friar Tuck, came over and I ordered a plate of sauerbraten. I hadn't eaten in nearly twelve hours. My stomach was tight with anxiety and tension. It was a feeling I hadn't had since the first time I repoed a car. I kept looking over my shoulder to see if the owner was about to come at me with a sledge hammer. I was also worried that someone might think I was heisting the car—well, I was, in a way.

I stared at the food for a few seconds, trying to muster up the proper enthusiasm. Finally, after swallowing a few forkfuls, I realized it wasn't working. I pushed the rest toward the edges of the plate and sat there for the next twenty minutes, mostly looking at my watch. When half an hour was up, I paid for the meal. The waiter gave me a dirty look. It was the kind of look the SS must have reserved for their concentration camp victims.

I went back to my room and dialed the Embassy. Stan Powers got on the line. "Did you get anything?" I asked him.

"You know, I wouldn't do this for just anybody."

"I know."

"Jeff said you were okay."

"It's nice to know people think you're okay."

"Well, he does. He also said you've got a pipeline to Knicks tickets. I get to the City sometimes."

"And you like the Knicks."

"I like basketball. And I like good seats."

"Done. So, what did you find out?"

"It looks like you got yourself mixed up with some very colorful characters."

"Yeah?"

"That's right. Seems this Joséf Doeppel fellow used to be an agent."

"For who?"

"You know, this could be a sticky situation."

"Jeff cleared me, didn't he?"

"Yeah, but..."

"Come on. If this guy was an agent, we're talking about a hundred years ago. If you could find it out, it can't be all that classified, can it?"

"Yeah, well, just don't go blabbing it around where you got it, that's all."

"You've got my word."

"Okay. It was for British Intelligence mostly, but he had some CIA connections, too. Recruited after the war. From what I could find, he had a reputation as a good man—up to a point, that is. Far as I could ascertain, he hasn't worked for the Agency in some time, at least not officially. Retired, though not necessarily voluntarily. There's some kind of cloud over him, but I can't say just what it is. His past is kind of hazy. I suppose that's the sign of a good agent, though. And remember, it's a very closed-mouthed fraternity he's a member of. The incident, if it was an incident, that got him kicked out or what have you, happened in the late '60s. From what I can find out, it had something to do with smuggled contraband art works stolen by the Nazis and then re-sold on the black market after the War.

"Look, I've got to tell you, we're dealing with a kind of underground community here that's completely removed from the real world. They have their own way of speaking, their own set of regulations, their own code of behavior, their own set of morals and their own rumors. If I had more time, I might be able to come up with something more concrete, but I couldn't promise it. There's a heavy lid on some things, and it isn't easy to pry something like that off once the intelligence community decides they don't want it to be public knowledge."

"So he might have been a Nazi working for the CIA and British Intelligence?"

"Like I told you, that's the way the world is sometimes. The CIA wouldn't care much about his past. It's something they'd use to their advantage. It's what the man can do for them now that counts. Listen, pal, in this business things sometimes get turned topsy-turvy. Pretty soon you don't know who's working for who. You don't even know who anyone is anymore. Trust is a word that's got all kinds of different meanings in the Intelligence dictionary, all according to the particular situation. Believe me, I'm glad I'm not mixed up in that stuff. Embassy work is tough enough. Anyway, the final word on Doeppel is that maybe he picks up a freelance assignment here and there, but, for the most part, he's out of the business. He's gotta be seventy-five years old, if he's a day."

"And Charles Martel?"

"There you've got a bigger fish. Used to be one of the other side's top agents. Went by the name of Horst Kleiner. Changed it to Martel when he went aboveground in '90, when the Wall came down. Don't know what he's involved with now, though."

"Have you got an address on him?"

"Sure, but I don't see how it's going to do you any good. You don't expect to waltz yourself over there, ring his bell, and get yourself invited in for a shot of schnapps, do you?"

"I want to send him a Christmas card, okay?"

"Okay, but if you get yourself in a jam, don't come crying to me. It's 27 Dresdenerstrasser. In the old eastern sector."

I jotted down the address. "How would I get there?"

"Oh, come on."

"Just the directions, please. I already got the warning."

"Take the U-Bahn to Kochstrasser. Then take the S-Bahn to Dresdenerstrasser. Now how about telling me what the hell this is all about?"

"Sorry."

"Hey, come on. What if something happens? You want

somebody watching your back, don't you?"

"You could help?"

"I'm not saying that."

"Very reassuring."

"I warned you."

"Yeah, you did. If I go, I'll go over tonight and should be back by morning. I'll give you a call then. If you don't hear from me, send in the cavalry."

"There is no cavalry, pal."

"Then send in anything you like. I've got one more favor to ask."

"This is getting tiresome."

"Don't worry, I'll return it someday. I'd like you to check on a few other names for me."

"Look, I've got other work to do."

"If things go the way I think, you'll be a hero."

"I'm not interested in being a hero. But okay, give me the names. If I have time, I'll check them for you."

"I'd appreciate it. Karl Egeleise, Wilhelm Doeppel, he's Joséf's nephew, and Harry Janus. See if you can come up with anything on them."

"Listen, Swann, I gotta tell you, this is some serious shit you're getting yourself into. This Martel had quite a reputation. He didn't fool around."

"Thanks for the comforting words."

I hailed a cab and took it to the U-Bahn. I was feeling good. The tightness in my stomach had eased and my head was slowly clearing. While on the platform I noticed a man in a light tan trench coat, standing about 30 feet down the line. He was apparently reading a newspaper, but it appeared he was watching me. I took a few steps closer to get a better look. He turned away from me. Before I could get any closer the train arrived. I got in and took a window seat. The man, still standing in the same spot, dropped his newspaper and watched as the train pulled out. I was pretty sure he was watching me.

A few minutes later, the train reached Kochstrasser, and I got off. I stood alone for a moment on the platform. I was a foreigner again, set adrift like a dinghy in the middle of the sea. Suddenly, I longed for some kind of identification with the familiar. Something to hold on to. I needed a friendly, familiar face, a recognizable landmark, a voice I knew. Standing on the edge of the train tracks, I thought of my son and was sorry that I hadn't spoken to him before leaving the States.

I looked around, trying to get my bearings, as the light was turning from day to night. I hurried toward the S-Bahn and headed in the direction of 27 Dresdenerstrasser and my unannounced appointment with Charles Martel. I tried not to think about what might happen. 🏃

# The Wizard
## OF AHS

I WAS STANDING UNDER the harsh yellow glare of a street lamp, gazing up at number 27 Dresdenerstrasser. It was one in a long line of carbon-copy brick buildings on the block. Each rose precisely six stories high and, although they had all been built during the post-War, their design appeared much older.

Something wasn't right about the whole set-up. The streets, for one thing, were completely empty. Though it was only a little past 8:00 p.m., it might as well have been two in the morning. Nothing stirred. I felt like I was standing in the midst of a vacuum.

From somewhere in the distance I heard the sound of a car motor. I looked down the street and spotted an automobile with a flashing red light on the roof moving slowly toward me. A pair of headlights penetrated the dense fog as small droplets of moisture danced in front of the beams of light. I didn't know what else to do, so I bolted up the stairs of number 27 and pressed myself against the outer lobby wall. The car, lights flashing, passed slowly. I exhaled slowly, trying to calm myself. My damp hands left a greasy smear on the smooth glass of the lobby door.

I stayed pressed to the wall for a minute or two before allowing myself to relax. I turned and saw a series of nameplates. The light was bad, with the single overhead bulb having burnt out long before my arrival. Squinting from half a foot away, I managed to make out the name MARTEL. I hesitated a moment, then rang the bell. A muffled voice came through the intercom. "Who is it?" it asked in German.

"Herr Martel?" I said in a voice husky with phlegm.

The voice immediately switched to English. "Yes. Who is it?"

"My name is Henry Swann. I'm an American. I've come concerning an old friend of yours, Wilhelm Doeppel."

The buzzer sounded almost immediately. I twisted the door handle and pushed my weight against the heavy wrought iron door. It gave way and I entered the vestibule. I looked up at the top of the second landing, where a man was waiting. Dressed in a pair of dark slacks and white turtleneck sweater, he had one arm thrown casually over the banister. Half way up the stairs, I saw that in his free hand he was holding a small silver pistol. I stopped.

"Please keep moving, Herr Swann. Do not be frightened. I will not shoot. These are my neighbors. My wife is inside. I would not be so rude as to startle them this late in the evening. This is only a precaution. Please." He motioned me forward with his pistol.

Near the top of the landing I missed a step and fell forward, coming dangerously close to Martel's gun.

"I'm sorry." I stuttered, trying to regain my balance. "Slipped."

Martel smiled kindly. "Of course. I understand. You are frightened and nervous. Please, let me help you." He stuffed the pistol in his pocket and offered me a hand.

"Thanks," I muttered with more than a little embarrassment. He didn't say anything; he just held onto my arm and guided me into his apartment. A woman, a pretty blonde in a flowered print housecoat, stood in the middle of a well-furnished living room.

"This is my wife, Gretchen. My dear..." He suddenly switched to German. All I could pick up was the word "coffee." She bowed slightly and left the room.

Martel appeared to be in his late forties. He was clean-shaven with closely cropped salt-and-pepper hair. He had a long nose and closely set eyes with bushy eyebrows. Despite this asceticism, he had an almost kindly look. "Please sit, Herr Swann. A smoke, perhaps?" he said, taking a cigar from his breast pocket. "Havanas. A benefit of open relations with a certain Caribbean nation," he said with a smile.

"No, thanks."

"I hope you don't mind if I do."

"Be my guest."

"Please, sit then. I have been expecting you."

"Expecting?"

"Yes. We ex-spies still have our sources, no?" He laughed, as he cut away the tip of his cigar. He put the butt in his mouth, rolled it around, wetting the tip, then lit up.

"Just what sources would those be?"

"It so happens, Herr Swann, that you know more than one old friend of mine."

"You mean Joséf Doeppel?"

"Yes. And one who no longer resides in Germany. One who found it better for his health and, let us say, his wealth, to leave this country some time ago."

"Egeleise."

Martel smiled but said nothing. I tried to suppress a smile as Martel's wife returned with a tray of coffee and small cakes. She set it in front of us.

"*Danke*," Martel said, rising to kiss his wife on the cheek. Just like Ozzie and Harriet, I thought. "She is a wonderful woman, Herr Swann. Unfortunately, she does not speak a word of English. Her father was a general in the German army. Are you married?"

"Not anymore," I said, dropping a lump of sugar in my coffee. I stirred it slowly with the tip of my spoon, feeling the grainy rectangle dissolve. I was anxious to know everything all at once, yet I resisted pushing too quickly. "I suppose I've been watched."

"That would be a valid assumption. Once a spy, always a spy. It is difficult, I'm afraid, to break old habits."

"There was a man following me today."

"If you saw him, then he did not do his job so well."

"How long have you been watching me?"

Martel shrugged.

"Since I got to Germany? Before?"

"Herr Swann, I do not know how you led your life before you came to Berlin, so how would I know if you were being watched?"

"I'm not going to get many straight answers, am I?"

"For some questions, there are no straight answers."

I hesitated. I didn't want to say the wrong thing. If Martel was Janus's killer or he had something to do with it, I'd probably wind up swimming underwater in the Rhine well past the time I could hold my breath. But a lie might do me just as much damage. Weighing the alternatives, I decided the truth would serve me best.

"I'm here to find Harry Janus's killer," I said.

"Harry Janus?"

"I believe you know him. After all, you were leaving messages for him all over New York, weren't you?"

"Was I?"

"And I think you also know that Harry Janus was your childhood buddy, Wilhelm Doeppel."

"Then I suppose Wilhelm Doeppel must be dead," he said coolly.

"That's right. But I think you knew that, didn't you?"

"You believe I had something to do with the death of this person, Harry Janus, who you say was my old friend, Wilhelm Doeppel."

"I didn't say that."

"Then what are you saying, Herr Swann?"

"I'm saying there's a good chance you might be able to lead me to the killer. It's not that I want to bring him to justice. I couldn't care less. I'm just a hired hand. I'm being paid to come up with an answer. It's very mercenary of me, but that's just the kind of guy I am. I can't seem to help myself. So all I need is an answer, and then I can go home and collect my money. Even a reason will do. I'm no moralist, Herr Martel. I'm just a working stiff trying to get along."

"Is money such a powerful motive for you, Herr Swann? Is there enough money in the world to die for?"

"I don't think I'd go quite that far."

"Then why get yourself involved in something that so obviously does not concern you? I assure you that if Doeppel is dead, his killer had reason, even if it does not ultimately make sense to you."

"Well, I'm here, so what say, just between you and me, we solve this thing?"

Martel smiled and chugged on his cigar. "You've taken quite a chance. If you have found your murderer, then you might not leave here alive.

"Like I said, I'm not accusing you of anything, and even if you were the one, it's not my job to bring you in. I just want the answer, that's all."

Martel sipped his coffee and flicked an ash onto a dish. "Very generous of you, Herr Swann. But the truth is I do not, as a rule, have old friends murdered." He drew long on his cigar and exhaled a cloud of smoke which, for a moment, obscured his face. "In the past, during the Cold War, I existed on the edge of a precipice. I worked to topple governments. But no longer. Now, I am one of you."

"What's that supposed to mean?" He smiled, but said nothing.

"You and your friend Egeleise make quite a pair."

He smiled. "We have certain things in common, but I would not call him a friend. Would you like a brandy?"

"Fine," I said, hoping it would take the chill off. My head ached and I felt a weakness behind my knees and at the back of my neck. Martel rose and moved to the bar. He poured a snifter of brandy for me and wine for himself. Returning with the glasses, he said, "Herr Egeleise and I have had some business dealings together. Certain treasures should be shared with the world, don't you think?" He raised his glass. "To your health, Herr Swann."

"I'll drink to that," I said, raising my glass in salute. My throat was dry. The brandy felt good going down. There didn't seem to be any heat in the flat and the dampness was beginning to cut right through me. I took another hit and said, "So you're in the art business, and I guess you see yourself as some kind of liberator?"

"Sarcasm, Herr Swann. Tsk, tsk, tsk." He waved a finger at me.

"How about Egeleise's Nazi connections?"

Martel seemed unperturbed. "I know directly of no such dealings."

"I think maybe you and Egeleise were in business together dealing stolen art and artifacts. And maybe Janus was your New York connection. Maybe he sold the goods for you."

Martel's face twisted into what might pass as a smile. I knew he was toying with me, but I went through with the charade of asking questions anyway, knowing full well that he'd tell me only what he wanted me to know. "You have a very active imagination. Certainly, we had some dealings together. Just what they were, I am not prepared to say."

"You know of his interest in the Peking Man?"

"He had an interest in archaeology. He talked of returning

to Egypt and the pyramids. It was purely academic, to satisfy his curiosity about the origins of man. He was a man obsessed by the occult. Anything beyond the explanation of man interested him. Even something as ridiculous as 'pyramid power' fascinated him. Rejuvenation under the pyramid, utter nonsense, but to him it was something to be investigated." Martel shook his head. "I am a man who believes only in what he can see and touch, but he was different."

"Did he try to interest you in the hunt for the Peking Man?"

"He thought I could help him deal with the Chinese."

"What kind of help did you give him?"

"He wanted information about a certain German woman."

"The woman who was supposed to know the whereabouts of the bones?"

"Yes."

"Did she?"

"Perhaps."

"This is what you told Doeppel?"

"I tried."

"What do you mean?"

"I could not reach him."

"You mean he was already dead?" He said nothing. "Do you think his death had something to do with this woman and the search for those bones?"

Martel sighed. Evidently, he was getting bored. "Herr Swann," he said, puffing on his cigar. "There are a thousand and one reasons for a man to die. Sometimes we know why, other times not."

"Aren't you interested in who killed your friend?"

"I was only marginally interested in his life, so why should I be interested in his death, which affects me not at all?"

"I don't understand your attitude."

"If the man is dead, there is nothing I can do to bring him back."

"If you have doubts of his death...."

"You are the one who tells me he had more than one life. If so...."

"Do you know who killed him or not?"

He didn't answer.

"Well, then, can you tell me the woman's name, the one he was looking for? Or what you found out about her?"

He shook his head, no.

"Have you ever had any dealings with a man in California named Jack Sharp or Schwartz?"

He smiled.

"Jason Cheney."

Another smile.

"Lucio Cabañas?"

"I would be lying if I did not admit to recognizing the name."

"As far as I can tell Cheney, Cabañas, Doeppel, Janus, were all names used by the same person."

Martel shrugged. "I knew little of Wilhelm's life after he left Germany. A man has many faces, many moods, many names, especially in my business. We were not in touch constantly. Only at various periods in our lives did our paths intersect."

"Like Mexico with Egeleise?"

Suddenly, I felt a strange sensation surging through my body, and then I couldn't feel my body at all. The room began to spin. I felt as if I were falling. I leaned back and grabbed hold of the arm of the couch, which was also spinning. I dropped my glass. Moments, maybe it was seconds, later, I heard the tinkle of breaking glass. I fought desperately to keep my eyes open and my head clear. I was hot, then cold. I gasped for air. Was I dying? A heart attack?

I listened for a heartbeat. At first it was not there at all, and then it was, louder and louder, faster and faster. My mind raced. Is this death? I wondered. My head started to fill with unrelated incidents from my past, and then, oddly enough, from the past of Harry Janus. I couldn't tell them apart. Had they happened to him or me...or both of us? I tried to connect them all, but it was a jumble. I tried to get my body to move, but it wouldn't.

Vaguely, as through a thick screen, I heard Martel's voice. "Only something to make you sleep. Any further conversation between us would be futile. Goodbye, Herr Swann." ⚲

# Getting Off,
## PLEASE

I AWOKE IN DARKNESS. I was lying on a bed of some sort, but I had no idea where it was. I thought back to the last place I'd been: Martel's apartment. Was I still there?

I blinked my eyes. Slowly, things came back into focus. I tried getting up, but couldn't. My body was heavy, immobile. I closed my eyes and listened intently for sounds. There were none. My head was clearing. I looked at my watch to see what time it was, but my eyes couldn't quite focus completely yet.

My head hurt and my mouth was dry. I tried to produce some saliva, but couldn't seem to manage what should have been a simple task. I was finally able to make it to a sitting position, using my hands to prop me up. I looked around, but couldn't see any thing in the dark. Blackness blacker than black. Enclosed in a room. A cell, perhaps? I focused on a spot in front and below me, trying to pick up even a hint of light. Just a thread. I could follow it then to more...light.

There was a string of light lying on the floor. I tried to focus on the source. Was it the bottom of a door? There were footsteps, padded, as if on carpet. I remained perfectly still.

The footsteps passed. I swung my legs off the bed and stood. I was woozy. I put my hands on the side of the bed to steady myself. Moving like a blind man, my hands out in front to protect against unseen objects, I made my way toward the string of light, my eyes riveted to the spot. I groped for what I hoped would be a doorknob. My hand felt cold metal. I grasped it firmly and twisted, very slowly, so as to make as little noise as possible. If I were to have any advantage at all, it had to be surprise. The knob turned easily. Seconds passed as I gripped the knob, waiting for just the right moment to go all the way. It was time. I turned. There was an almost inaudible click. The door moved toward me. Suddenly, more light filled the room, adding hints of color to the blackness. I opened it a few inches and peered out.

I was back in my hotel room at the Hilton.

Confused, dazed, I went to the window and drew back the curtains. It was still night. I looked at my watch: 4:00 a.m. What morning? How had I gotten back to the room?

In the bathroom, I gazed at myself in the mirror and was startled by what I saw. My face was gaunt, practically colorless. With six days' growth of beard, I looked so much older than I had a week before. I bore little resemblance to the self I was back in New York. My hands shook. I splashed water on my face, then returned to the room and sat on the edge of the bed. Elbows on my thighs, I cradled my head in my hands and slowly massaged my temples.

Quick images of what I'd been through in the past week flashed through my mind. I wiped my face with the sleeve of my shirt and leaned back on the bed as I tried to sort things out. But every time I thought I was moving ahead in a straight line, my mind wandered off and I had to start all over again. This wasn't working, so I grabbed a pen and pad from the nightstand with the intention of writing things down. But I just sat there, staring out into space. I tried to focus my eyes on the wall, across the room, hoping that would help me center myself. It worked for a while, but then I drifted off again, thinking about Martel and Doeppel and Sally Janus. And then my mind would jump to something else, something totally unconnected—my wife, my son, shreds of a life that I knew was going nowhere. I had to solve this case or I would simply disintegrate and disappear from the face of the earth, a lost man on a lost continent on what might be a lost cause, with no one to search for him. ⚡

# More
# LOOSE ENDS

T HE TELEPHONE RANG as I was lethargically packing what little I had into my small bag. It was Stan Powers. "Swann, glad to see you made it back in one piece. Find what you were looking for?"

"More or less."

"Listen, I've got something for you. It's hot stuff. I don't even know if I should be telling it to you."

Suddenly, I could feel my body energize. Maybe, just maybe, what Stan had to tell me would help clear things up a little, lift this low, oppressive cloud from above my head.

"Stop jerking me around, Stan. You know you can't wait to tell me what you've got."

"Okay, okay, but this is worth at least a couple Knicks games, and good seats, too. First of all, this Egeleise turns out to have a very shady past."

"That doesn't surprise me."

"Well, would it surprise you to know that the German government is looking for him?"

"Why?"

"Because he's a Nazi war criminal, that's why. He's on the list. The last time anyone spotted him was down in Argentina more than fifteen years ago. There've been a lot of rumors concerning his whereabouts, but nothing concrete. The Israelis have been looking for him. Rumor has it he's in Mexico, or maybe Nicaragua. He's supposed to be very active in Odessa. That's the secret, worldwide organization that's supposed to protect Ex-Nazis. Any way, Egeleise, whose real name is Braun, is one ofthe big moneymen. Supposedly, he's a conduit for art stolen during the War. A lot of that loot was taken out of Russia during the war and they wouldn't mind getting it back. Have you got a line on Egeleise?"

"Not a clue," I lied. The last thing I wanted to get involved with was helping in the hunt for Nazi war criminals. I had enough on my hands.

"Too bad. There's a connection between Egeleise and Joséf Doeppel. They were friends during and before the War. I don't have too much more on that, though. Now, here it gets a little more interesting and a little more complicated. Wilhelm Doeppel was a friend of Charles Martel, who was named Kleiner. And Joséf Doeppel was a pal of Egeleise, who was Braun. And Joséf is Wilhelm's uncle. Is this making any sense?"

"Some."

"Listen, are you going to be in Berlin much longer? I thought maybe we could get together for dinner or something and talk this out a little more."

"Sorry. I'm leaving later this morning. Got to get back home. Thanks for your help. When you get back to the States, look me up and those Knicks tix will be waiting."

I sat there on the edge of the bed for some minutes after I hung up. I was tempted to try and piece together the information

Powers had given me. But I resisted. I didn't have the heart for it at that moment. But I was pretty sure that now, finally, I had most of the pieces I needed to finish the puzzle. But I needed a clear head and familiar surroundings to do it.

At the airport, I stopped off at the souvenir shop and picked up a few items for the boys back at the Paradise Bar and Grill. I figured it was the least I could do, what with me being away for a week and not even sending them as much as a card. 🏃

# BACK IN
# NEW YORK

*Berlin to New York*

# Did
# You Ever See
## A DREAM WALKING?

I HAD PLENTY TO THINK about on the plane ride back home and, though I tried not to, it was unavoidable. I had examined another man's life—or tried to—through a lens that was cracked and out of focus. I came searching for an answer and left with only questions—questions about a man whose only verifiable fact was that he was dead.

I went back to basics, starting with the motives for murder. Money, jealousy, politics, revenge, shame. In Janus's case any one of those could have fit, but for some reason I kept coming back to money. And the source of the money in this case was looted art and artifacts. Janus, Martel and Egeleise were all tied together by their history and perhaps they were in business together. Partners. And perhaps one or even two partners got greedy. Perhaps Janus stole from Martel and Egeleise, and so they had him killed. Or perhaps Janus found that Martel and Egeleise were stealing from him, and when they found out he knew they had him killed.

There were all kinds of permutations. Which one was the right one?

The plane touched down at Kennedy at four-thirty Sunday afternoon. I emerged bleary-eyed. It was raining, the sky thick with dark, gray clouds that could have been the same ones that had covered East Berlin. It seemed no matter where I went, I always seemed to wind up back in the same place.

Once I got out of the terminal I was lost. I didn't know what to do, where to go. I needed to make contact with a familiar human being. But the only one I could think of at the moment was Sally Janus.

She was home. The first thing out of her mouth was, "They've solved the case. They've got Harry's killer."  ⚡

# The Final
# SOLUTION

THERE WAS A PART OF ME that didn't want to believe Harry Janus's killer had been caught. After all I'd been through, I wanted to be the one who found the killer. After all, I was the one who'd put in all the heavy lifting. And I was the one who had the aches and pains to prove it.

I was pretty wired up by the time I arrived at the Janus house. Sally Janus, looking good as ever, was watching a movie on her giant projection TV screen. "How about some popcorn?" she asked.

I declined.

"I've got some going right now."

"Maybe for the second feature."

"This movie is really terrific. Have you seen it? The Thomas Crown Affair."

"I'm not much for flicks, especially crime flicks."

"I can fill you in. It just started."

"No thanks. Think you can tear yourself away for a while?"

"No problem," she said. "I'll just tape it and catch it later." She pressed a couple buttons on the console and the film disappeared from the screen.

"You look terrible," she said, as if seeing me for the first time. "For one thing, you could use a shave."

I touched my face. "Yeah, well, I've been through a lot." "Yes, and I want you to know how much I appreciate it. I haven't forgotten about the money I owe you. Before you leave, remind me, and I'll give you a check. Of course, you'll have to wait until next week to cash it."

"I'm not worried about that right now."

"That's out of character, Swann. I thought it was all about the money for you. But you want to know the whole story, don't you?"

"Yeah. I do. Let's just take a seat here on the couch, munch on some popcorn, and you can tell me all about it."

"What's wrong with you?"

"With me?"

"Yes. You're being...sarcastic."

"Really? Well, maybe I'm just a little confused as to why you're taking this so matter-of-factly. Somehow, I get the feeling that the fact that they've found your husband's killer is more important to me than it is to you, and that's not the way it should be, is it?"

"Are you accusing me of being callous? Or superficial? Or uncaring?"

"Look, I'm tired and I ache all over, so why don't we just get this over with."

"I don't think I like your tone."

"Well, I'm afraid you're going to have to live with it."

She pouted a moment, waiting for me to apologize, I guess. But when she saw that that wasn't going to happen, she said, "Where should I begin?"

"Christ...."

"Okay. Detective Kelly called me yesterday and asked me to come downtown. He said he had information about Harry's murder."

"So?"

"So, I went downtown."

"Yeah?"

"You know, I loved him."

"Yeah."

"He had another life."

"He had many lives."

"He wasn't exactly what...who...I thought."

"Yes, well, I'd say that's pretty perceptive. But let's get back to the subject. Who killed him? Why? And how did the cops solve the case?"

"It was an accident."

"His murder was an accident?"

"No. The way the cops found his killer. That was the accident. They arrested someone for trying to shoot someone else. The ballistics matched. That's how they found him."

"Who was he?" I asked, maybe expecting to hear a familiar name.

"A nut. No one knows why he did it. There didn't seem to be any particular reason. He didn't know Harry. The police seem to think that maybe he was a serial killer in the making. A David Berkowitz kind of thing...you know, hearing voices."

"What was your husband doing down there?"

"That's what I mean about having another life. He was down there a lot, apparently."

"Doing what?"

"What do you think? He liked it. He would pick up women and take them...I really can't talk about this."

"Let me get this straight. Your husband liked taking hookers up to sleazy hotel rooms. He liked palling around with junkies, dope dealers and other lowlives."

"I guess so," she said, her voice lowering.

"And this time he just happened to be in the wrong place at the wrong time?"

"Uh-huh."

"And you're convinced this is the truth?"

"Yes."

"That's not what you thought a week or so ago."

"Well, now I'm convinced. How could I not be. The guy confessed."

"There's got to be more. There's something you're not telling me."

She looked me in the eye. "Why would I lie? I'm the one who hired you, remember?"

She was right. But there was something inside my skeptical brain that wasn't satisfied. The solution couldn't be so easy, so pat. Not after all I'd been through, after all I'd found out.

"I want to see him."

"Who?"

"The murderer."

"Why would you want to do that?"

"There's something about this that bothers me. It couldn't have been just a random act. There was a reason your husband was murdered, and it wasn't because he was a run-of-the-mill pervert in the wrong place at the wrong time."

"Suit yourself. You probably know where to find him."

"Yes, I do." I lingered a moment. There was some unfinished business, but for the life of me I couldn't think what it was.

"I don't know what to say, Swann. Just tell me what I owe you."

Yes, that was it.

THE SUSPECT, KENNETH BUTLER, had a public defender, who arranged for me to see his client, who was waiting for arraignment on Rikers Island. I told him I had been investigating the case and didn't believe his Butler was guilty.

That seemed to do the trick.

The next morning, as I was leaving my apartment to catch the bus to Rikers, I noticed someone following me. He looked suspiciously like the guy who had been trailing me in New York a week earlier. This time, rather than avoid him, I decided to intercept him. I led him to a nearby building that I knew had a back entrance and then I doubled back and grabbed him as he waited for me out front.

"Hey, pal, something I can do for you?" I asked, pushing him up against the wall of the building.

"Hey, what's going on?"

"I'll tell you what's going on. I want to know why you're following me."

"You're crazy. I'm not following you."

I patted him down for a weapon, but he didn't have one. I grabbed his wallet.

"Hey!"

"Relax, pal."

I opened it and started looking through it. "Who sent you? Was it Martel? Egeleise?" I pushed my elbow into his back as I continued looking through his wallet. Stuffed behind his cash I found a folded piece of paper. I took it out and opened it up. There was a phone number. It looked familiar, but I couldn't quite place it.

"Egeleise sent you, didn't he?"

Silence.

"We're three thousand miles away from him. You only have to worry about me now, pal." I pressed my elbow deeper into his back.

"I've got nothing to say."

"Well, the laugh's on him. Doeppel's dead. And whatever business they had together is over. Why don't you tell him that when you speak to him." I shoved the piece of paper into his pocket.

"I don't know what the hell you're talking about."

I didn't bother to explain it to him. Why should I? It didn't matter anymore. I was sure that after he spoke to his boss, I'd never see him again. So I let him go.

ᗑ

ON THE BUS OUT TO RIKERS, my head so much clearer than it had been the day before, I started to put the pieces together. Egeleise was in it from the beginning. He was just using me to find Janus or Doeppel or whatever the hell his name was. I was his puppet, and who knew what he'd done to manipulate me. Was he behind the attack on me in the hotel room? Was he behind the two hoods in L.A.? Or maybe it was his partner, Martel. And what was Jack Sharp's role in all this? Well, maybe he was part of their scheme involving the stolen art and artifacts. And maybe he was the one who hired those men to follow me and then beat up on me. And what about the death of Mike Pitts and the rest of the Argonauts? Well, maybe that was just a coincidence. After all, people die all the time... and the life expectancy of rock musicians isn't all that long anyway. And maybe Carole Cheney Sharp was just using all that to manipulate me, to make me think that she was in trouble, to keep me on the case. At least that's what I was thinking.

ᗑ

AT RIKERS, THEY BROUGHT IN KENNETH BUTLER. He sat opposite me, a glass partition separating us. We looked at each other for some time without exchanging a word. He was not what I'd expected. For one thing, he was small. Maybe five-six or seven. And thin. Very thin. You could put two fingers around his waist. He had a studious look. He was the kind of guy you might find hanging around a library, not a sleazy, Times Square hotel. He had a pinched face, close-cropped sandy hair, and a long, thin nose. He wore wire-rimmed glasses. He had a sad, forlorn look about him. There was something about him that seemed familiar, but I couldn't put my finger on it. His lawyer told me that he was "peculiar." I asked him what that meant. He said I'd see for myself. He was right.

I said, "Hello." He didn't respond. I looked him in the eye. He didn't blink. I told him my name. It didn't faze him. I asked him if he knew who I was. He didn't answer, but I could tell that he'd never seen me before. I asked him if he knew why he was there. A smile began to cross his face, but before it got far he stopped it. I asked him, "Did you kill Harry Janus?"

For the first time he spoke. "I prefer not to answer that question at this time." His voice was calm, though cold and detached. His mouth moved and the words tumbled out, but there was nothing behind them, no feeling, no sense of understanding. Just words.

"Why did you kill him?"

"I prefer not to answer at this time," he said.

I tried again. "Did someone else kill him?"

"I prefer not to answer at this time."

"Was someone else involved?"

Silence.

I was about to pack it in, but a little voice, call it instinct, kept telling me this wasn't over yet. I looked at Butler closer. A slight smile seemed to be forming at the corner of his mouth.

"You know me, don't you?"

"Why should I?"

"Because I know you."

"Really."

"You followed me to the Metropolitan Hotel a couple of weeks ago."

"I did?"

"Yes..." I stopped. The wheels were turning. Suddenly, I was making all kinds of connections. And this time I think they were taking me somewhere.

"You were hired to do this murder, weren't you? And you were hired to follow me."

Silence.

It didn't really matter. I finally had the answers, even if he preferred not to give them to me.

On the way back to Manhattan, I suddenly realized why he looked so familiar: he was a dead ringer for Lee Harvey Oswald.  🕴

# The Final
## FINAL SOLUTION

I BANGED ON THE DOOR till she opened it.

"Swann, what are you doing back here?"

"Unfinished business."

"I can't imagine what that might be, unless you're looking to get paid."

"Let me in."

"I really can't talk long, Swann. I've got an appointment," she said as she opened the door.

"This won't take long," I said, as I followed her into the living room. "You know, Sally, if I had a higher opinion of myself I might feel really bad about all this." She sat on the couch and I sat across from her.

"What's that supposed to mean?"

I leaned in closer. "You used me."

"Of course I used you. I paid you. You worked for me."

"But you didn't pay me for what I was really doing. You weren't interested in who killed your husband. You were interested in finding out as much about his life as you could."

"Why would I care?"

"Because you were interested in the money. You knew about your husband's dealings with Egeleise and Martel. You just didn't know who they were or where they were. You knew one of them had him killed—probably because he ripped them off—but you needed me to find them, so you could take your husband's place on the board of directors."

"I don't know what you're talking about."

"Sure you do. I realized that there must have been a connection when I remembered that photograph you showed me, the one you wouldn't let me keep. I told you that Carole Cheney looked familiar and the reason is that the redhead in the photo was her, which meant that you knew her, which meant that you knew more about your husband's life before he met you then you let on. Once I made that connection, I was able to start to put the links in the chain together. The three of them—Harry, Egeleise and Martel—were dealing in stolen art, much of it smuggled out of Germany after the war, some of it smuggled out of Mexico. I noticed the art auction house catalogues upstairs, and the same ones were in Egeleise's study. That's how they established values for the artwork they were fencing. I wouldn't be surprised if Carole's husband, Jack, wasn't involved in disposing of some of it. And I suspect that Harry, who seemed to be desperate for money, tried to rip them off in some way—because he was desperate for money to lay his hands on the Peking Man, which would make him famous. The others weren't interested in fame; all they cared about was the money. Harry was out of control, and because of that they had him killed. And when that happened, you were cut off. Living like this," I waved my arm around, "can be very addictive, can't it? So you wanted in. And the only way you could get in was to find out exactly who was involved and how things worked.

That's where I came in. You figured someone like me wouldn't ask any questions, he'd just do the job for the dough. And I was used to finding people, that's what I do for a living. It was the perfect plan. You didn't give a shit about who killed Harry. You just wanted to have me lead you to the source of the money."

I looked at her, hoping for some kind of confession, but her face was stone.

"Once I figured that out, everything else started to fall into place. I wondered how those people who were following me—the guy here in New York, the two thugs in L.A., always seemed to know where I was. Well, the only one who could have known that was you. You sold me out, lady."

"I didn't do anything wrong."

"Not unless you call hiring thugs to work me over doing something wrong."

"Why would I want to harm you?"

"To keep me going. You figured I might need an incentive, beyond the money, I mean. Funny thing is, I didn't. I would have done it just for the dough. That's the kind of guy I am. You know, in the end, and it hurts me to admit it, even if it is true, we have more in common than you might have thought. The difference is, I have limits."

"I was his wife. He left me nothing...."

"So what makes you think you're any better off now? What kind of leverage do you think you have with Martel and Egeleise?"

She fidgeted with her necklace.

"The answer is, you don't have any. I don't suppose it matters, but I have to warn you, Sally, you're dealing with dangerous men here. If I were you, I'd drop it. Pick up the chips you have left—this house, for instance—and walk away."

She got up, as she fidgeted with a chain around her neck. "I think you better go now."

"Yeah, I think that's what I'll do. And you know something, I think I will take what you owe me. That is, if you're around long enough to cover the check."

"You don't have to worry about me."

"No, I don't suppose I do. But still, I'd watch my back, if I were you."

She wrote me out a check and I folded it up and put it in my wallet without looking at it. I got up. I walked to the door and she followed. "Swann, I want you to know, I had absolutely nothing to do with Harry's death."

"You know something, I believe you, but it doesn't matter. When it comes right down to it, you're just as guilty as they are. You were both using Harry. He was no angel, from what I know about him, but he did have a conscience. I'm not sure about the rest of you."

Outside, I opened my wallet and unfolded the check. I smiled. It was for half the amount she owed me. Oh, well, I thought, easy come, easy go.

As I walked away, I kept repeating the names Janus, Doeppler, Cheney, over and over again until it finally hit me. What did they all have in common? They weren't random choices on Wilhelm Doeppler's part. Multiplicity, that's what it was. Doeppler, like doeppelganger; Janus, two-faced; Cheney, Lon Cheney, the Man of a Thousand Faces. I smiled. Doeppler was playing his own little joke. That's what he was doing. Only in the end, the joke was on him...because he was dead, and no matter how many people he might have been in life, now he was just a single corpse lying in a grave somewhere.

A few hours later, I was comfortably ensconced back in my regular seat at the Paradise Bar and Grill. I had a little extra money in my pocket—not much, but a little—and I meant to spend it. I'd worry about the future later...when it didn't matter anymore.

Right then, though, I was the hit of the party. The boys were actually glad to see me. And why not? I was spending money like it was going out of style. I was having such a good time that I even let myself get talked into reciting a little po-it-tree. And why not. After all, as someone a lot wiser than me once said, "Life is short, art is long."

"Come on, Swann," Manny urged, "give us one of them poems that don't make no sense but sound good."

"My specialty," I said, and I launched into one.

*Here is little Effie's head*
*Whose brains are made of gingerbread.*
*When the judgment day comes*
*God will find six crumbs....*

And when I ended with,

*Cross the threshold have no dread,*
*Lift the sheet back in this way.*
*Here is little Effie's head*
*Whose brains are made of gingerbread*

The bar erupted in cheers, Manny slapped me on the back and shoved another cold one into my hand, Joe Bailey, who'd come in from the back room, gave me the high sign, and I knew I was back where I belonged.

Just before I was ready to call it a night, someone popped a quarter into the jukebox, and what should come up but a song called "Stomp Out the Fires of My Heart." And you know what, I didn't even give it a second thought. Instead, I just hoisted one last beer in honor of Harry Janus. And the funny thing was, the rest of the boys at the Paradise Bar and Grill did the same.

And they didn't even know him from Adam. ⚑

# Selling Out
## SWANN

*A version of this essay appeared in the February 2009 issue of*
Writer's Digest.

YEARS AGO, I WROTE A NOVEL called *Swann's Last Song*.
Only now is it being published. And only because I was
finally, after three decades, during which time it resided
in a file cabinet, tucked inside a hardly opened storage closet,
willing to compromise. Or, let's call it what it really is: I sold out.

The idea, I thought, was rather simple and it came to me as
I was in the midst of a reading jag of classic detective and crime
fiction: Hammett, Chandler, Cain, MacDonald. It wasn't so
much about being attracted to the mystery, although there was
something neat and tidy in having the detective, that noirish,
troubled anti-hero, wrap up the case, then head out to the
nearest bar and tie one on. At least that's the way I imagined it. It
was more about the necessity, in those kinds of novels, to adhere

to a strict plotline, something I wasn't used to doing. Instead, I was more drawn to character—in fact, an MFA writing professor at Columbia once admonished me for writing "psychological crap like Dostoevsky, Nabokov and Bellow." I took that as a compliment, and not only dropped the class but opted out of the program, winding up making a living in magazine journalism.

The first detective story that fascinated me, kept me awake at nights in fact, was Poe's "The Murders in the Rue Morgue." It was read to us at summer camp by counselors, in nightly installments which, in retrospect, was probably simply a ploy to keep us in line or else we wouldn't hear the end. Days were spent trying to figure out who committed the murder, and when the startling secret was finally revealed, there was a sense that all was finally right with the world. Later, I realized that is really what detective fiction is all about: putting the world in order. Or, as literary critic, Michael Wood once wrote, "All detective fiction is fairly theological, given to displays of ultimate coherence..."

But what if the world weren't that way? What if it were messy? Random? Chaotic? Nonsensical? What if the pieces didn't fit?

After all, in the early 1970s, the world was anything but coherent. We were trying to extricate ourselves from a war that it seemed no one but our government wanted. We were still getting over the assassination of John F. Kennedy, his brother, Bobby, and Martin Luther King, Jr. Charles Manson had somehow mesmerized a group of hippy misfits into killing sprees. What's more, all kinds of conspiracy theories were afloat. We were certain that Lee Harvey Oswald did not act alone. And how could a redneck, low-I.Q. drifter like James Earl Ray possibly have committed that murder without help?

In the midst of my reading, I came across this passage from Ross MacDonald's *The Instant Enemy*: "I had to admit to myself that I lived for nights like these, moving across the city's great broken body, making connections among its millions of cells. I had a crazy wish or fantasy that some day before I died, if I made all the right neural connections, the city would come all the way alive. Like the Bride of Frankenstein."

That's all I needed to jolt me into action. What if those neural connections were made and the city didn't come alive?

Writers try to make sense of the world. Our own inner world and the world around us. Just like the classic detective. But my idea was to write a literary, anti-detective novel or, as a friend of mine put it, "an existential detective novel." People, I imagined, would be lulled into thinking they were reading a typical mystery but would then be jolted into realizing it was something more, a literary novel of ideas disguised as something they thought they recognized: the classical, American detective novel.

But for that to work, I had to come up with a plot that made sense. And a protagonist, the "detective," clever enough to follow clues, while being entertaining—the reader had to root for him to solve the crime—and, if I could manage it, "different," an outsider trying to get in.

I had recently written a magazine article on a skip tracer, someone who finds people who've skipped on their bills, or their spouse, and so I decided to use that profession—a finder of lost things, someone eminently capable of finding a trail and following it—for my anti-hero, Henry Swann.

I knew it was necessary to "borrow" the usual detective fiction conventions. Beautiful woman hires detective to look for her missing husband. But almost immediately, I turned that conceit on its head by having Swann, a money-grubbing loser who worked out of a small office in Spanish Harlem, find that the man had been murdered in a sleazy Times Square Hotel, thus effectively putting him out of a job. But the wife disagrees with the police verdict that he was killed by a pimp during a liaison gone bad and hires Swann to find the real killer. That quest takes the cynical Swann halfway around the world as he follows clues that lead him to find that the dead man had several different identities and led several different, lives: a

California rock star, a Mexican rebel, a German spy. And I made sure that just about each and every conspiracy theory out there was milked for all it was worth.

The novel ended with Swann, exhausted, confused, disillusioned, and no closer to the solution of the crime. But, as it turns out, the police come up with the perpetrator (whom I named Butler, for obvious reasons) and, as it happens, the crime was totally random, having nothing at all to do with all the clues Swann has so carefully collected and followed.

My agent loved the book. Until she reached the end.

"You can't do that," she said. "It's a genre book and readers expect the detective to solve the crime. If he doesn't, then they're disappointed."

"And that's bad?" I said.

"Yes, that's bad. Change the ending."

"I can't do that," I said, standing on the principles that, up to then, had gotten me nowhere.

I didn't want to give up, so I submitted it to an editor I'd worked with. She loved the book. And she got it. But when she showed it to her colleagues, they said, "He can't do that. We'll consider it, if he'll change the ending."

No, I would not change the ending. That would make the whole premise of the book disappear. I was young. I had my principles. I held to them.

So the book languished in that file cabinet for over twenty years. And then, one day, while cleaning out the closet, I came across the manuscript and started to read. It was surprisingly good. It held up. Times were different, I thought. I was a published author now. Maybe if I changed a few things, updated it, I could get it published after all.

So that's what I did. And when it was finished, I showed it to an agent and he said, "This is really good, but you can't keep this ending." I showed it to an editor at M. Evans whom I worked with and she said, "I really like this, but that ending."

I swallowed hard. "What if I changed it?"

"In that case, we might be interested in publishing it."

The wheels started turning. Whereas twenty-five years ago I had principles, I'd long since lost those—much like my protagonist, Swann, by the way. Why waste a perfectly good story? Maybe I could work something out that would save my original idea, and yet satisfy the readers. And so I came up with what I thought was a compromise I could live with (in fact, it wasn't a compromise at all—let's call it what it was, a complete and utter capitulation). I handed in the new ending and the people at M. Evans were pleased. "We'll publish it."

Like any good detective novel, the story never ends where you think it will. And this one doesn't either.

*Swann's Last Song* was scheduled to be released in May 2006. I got the galleys and cover art in the fall of 2005. It looked terrific. Finally, after all these years, it was going to be published. But not so fast. A month or two later M. Evans was swallowed up by another publisher, one that did little fiction and certainly not genre fiction. I was an orphan. I had the book with a changed ending, but no publisher. The file cabinet beckoned.

My agent sent it out to other publishers and it was picked up by Five Star Press, who had no idea of the original ending but was obviously comfortable with the new one.

And so, in September, with a new cover, *Swann's Last Song* will finally see the light of day. I have no second thoughts. No guilt. I can sleep at night. And what I've learned, if anything, is that although life can be messy and chaotic and unpredictable, detective fiction cannot.

*What follows, for anyone who's interested, is the original, or as I like to think of it, "lost" last chapter.* ⚔

# The Final
# SOLUTION

I TRIED NOT TO THINK ABOUT ANY OF IT as I rode a cab into the city. Fat chance of that. How can I explain how I felt? Relieved. Curious. Angry. Frustrated. Confused. Anxious. Inadequate.

But most of all, I had this fist in the pit of my stomach that told me I wasn't going to like what I heard. There was a part of me that didn't want to believe Harry Janus's killer had been caught. Frankly, I would have preferred his murder remain one of life's mysteries, like where old socks disappear to in the dryer.

I was even prepared to disbelieve whatever solution awaited me. After everything I'd been through, how could anyone else possibly have solved the crime?

I was all wired up by the time I arrived at the Janus house. Sally Janus, looking good as ever, was watching some movie on her giant projection TV screen. "How about some popcorn?" she asked.

I declined.

"I've got some going right now."

"Not now...maybe for the second feature."

"This movie is really terrific. Have you seen it?"

I squinted at the screen. "I don't even know what it is."

"It's the one with Robert Redford and Faye Dunaway. I forget the name of it."

"I'm not much for flicks."

"You don't know what you're missing. I can fill you in. It just started."

"No thanks. Think you can tear yourself away for a while?"

"No problem," she said. "I'll just tape it and catch it later." She pressed a couple buttons on the console and the film disappeared from the screen.

"You look terrible," she said, as if seeing me for the first time.

"Yeah, well, I've been through a lot. And I guess you know why."

She put her hand on my face and kissed me. "Yes, and I want you to know how much I appreciate it. I haven't forgotten about the money I owe you. Before you leave, remind me, and I'll give you a check. Of course, you'll have to wait until next week to cash it."

"I'm not worried about that right now."

"That's out of character, Swann. But you want to know the whole story, don't you?"

"Sure. Let's just take a seat here on the couch, munch on some popcorn, and you can tell me all about it."

"What's wrong with you?"

"With me?"

"Yes. You're being sarcastic."

"Excuse me. It's just you're taking this so matter-of-factly. Somehow, I think this is more important to me than it is to you, and that's not the way it should be, is it?"

"Are you accusing me of being callous? Or superficial?"

"Look, I'm tired and I ache all over, so why don't we just get this over with."

"Where should I begin?"

"Christ."

"Okay. It happened yesterday. Detective Kelly called and asked me to come downtown. He said he had information about Harry's murder."

"So?"

"So, I went downtown."

"Yeah?"

"You know, I loved him."

"Yeah, well, as it happens a lot of people seemed to feel that way...at least for a while."

"He had another life."

I laughed. "Tell me about it."

"He wasn't exactly what...who...I thought."

"Yes, well, I'd say that's a pretty perceptive observation. But let's get back to the subject. Who killed him? Why? And how did the cops solve the case?"

"It was an accident."

"His murder was an accident?"

"No. The way the cops found his killer. That was the accident. They arrested someone for trying to shoot someone else. The ballistics matched. That's how they found him."

"Who was he?" I asked, maybe expecting to hear a familiar name.

"Just some guy going around killing people. He was a nut. He'd hang out around Times Square and watch the hookers. Apparently, he got violent and started killing people. No one knows why."

"This doesn't make sense. What was your husband doing down there?"

"That's what I mean about having another life. He was down there a lot, apparently."

"Doing what?"

"What do you think? He liked it. Everyone knew who he

was. I mean, they didn't really know who he was, but they knew him."

I was hearing all this, but I wasn't quite believing or comprehending it. "Let me get this straight. Your husband liked hanging out in Times Square. He liked taking hookers up to a sleazy hotel room and fucking their brains out. He liked palling around with junkies, dope dealers and other scuzzy types. Am I getting this straight?"

"I guess so," she said, her voice lowering.

"And he just happened to be in the wrong place at the wrong time?"

"Uh-huh."

"And you're convinced this is the truth?"

"Yes."

"I don't believe you. I don't believe it. There's more. There's something you're not telling me."

She looked me in the eye. "Why would I lie? What do I have to gain? I'm the one who hired you, remember? I'm telling you, this is the truth."

"You knew him. Why do you think he led that kind of life?"

She shrugged. "You never really know what goes on in someone's head. Anyway, does it really matter?"

"It does to me."

"Would you like me to make something up?"

I glared at her. Suddenly, I didn't like her much anymore. I didn't respect her, either. How could she be so calm, so dispassionate? Wasn't she curious? Didn't she want to know the answers?

"I can, you know. I can tell you all about how when he was a kid he wasn't loved, wasn't accepted, didn't feel part anything. I could tell you about his insecurities and his poor self-image. I could do all that, you know."

"But it wouldn't be the truth."

"How do we know. Maybe it would. Does all that sound so outrageous? It could be the truth, couldn't it? I'm not going to go through the rest of my life blaming myself, if that's what you want. What Harry was he was a long time before I ever met him. I didn't drive him to the kind of life he led. I didn't push him into some hotel room where he got killed. It happened, that's all."

She was right. But there was something inside me that wasn't satisfied. There was a part of me that couldn't believe it could be so easy, so pat. "What was the guy's name?"

"Who?"

"The killer."

"Kenneth Butler."

I laughed. I couldn't help myself.

"Why are you laughing?"

"You don't get it?"

"No."

"The name."

"What about it?"

"It's absurd."

"What's so absurd about Kenneth Butler?"

I laughed again. "You really don't get it, do you?"

"No."

"The Butler did it."

"Oh," she said.

"You don't find that…ironic…absurd?"

"I suppose, under other circumstances, it might be funny. But it's just a silly coincidence, isn't it?"

"I suppose it is. Did you see him?"

"No. Why would I want to do that?"

"I don't know, but I want to see him. I want to touch him. I want to make sure he's real."

She shrugged. "Suit yourself. You know where to find him."

"Yes, I do." I lingered a moment. There was some unfinished business, but for the life of me I couldn't think what it was.

"Well?"

"This is it, huh?"

"I don't know what to say, Swann. The thing that brought us together, well, it's over now."

"I suppose it is. I guess we got carried away there for a minute."

"Tell me what I owe you."

"We're even. The books are closed."

"If I owe you something, I want to pay. I told you about that insurance money."

"Like I said, we're even. So, I guess this is goodbye."

"I suppose it is. Well, thank you," she said, offering me her hand. I shook it because what else was I supposed to do with it? I was going to ask her if she wanted me to get back in touch with her if I found out anything else, but I didn't. If there was anything else to know, she certainly didn't want to know it. And maybe that's the way it should have been...for her.

When I left Sally Janus, I called Kelly and found that the suspect was out on Rikers Island. He had a public defender. I got in touch with him and arranged to see his client. Supposedly, he wasn't talking, but I wanted to see for myself. I wanted to see him. I wanted to look into his eyes. I wanted to know if he really was the one.

The next morning, as I was leaving my apartment to catch the bus to Rikers, I noticed someone following me. It seemed to me it was the same man who'd been trailing me in New York a week earlier and maybe even the one who was in Germany with me. This time, I decided to find out for sure. I led him to a building with a back entrance, and then I doubled back and grabbed him as he waited for me out front.

"Can I do something for you?" I asked, pushing him up against a building.

"What do you want?" he asked.

"I want to know why you're following me."

"I'm not."

"Listen, pal, I'm gonna call the cops if you don't tell me, so you might as well. Who sent you?" I felt his body for weapons.

He didn't have any. "Was it Martel?" There was no response and his expression remained unchanged. Fear. "How about Egeleise?" His jaw tightened. I knew he'd been sent by Egeleise. I asked him why.

"I can't say."

"I'm not about to tell anybody. You can trust me. We're three thousand miles away. You only have to worry about me, pal."

"He wants Doeppel. He hired me to follow you to get to Doeppel."

"The laugh's on him, pal. Doeppel's dead. I told him that and it's true."

"He doesn't believe it. Look, I'm just a hired hand. He called me about a week ago and asked me to keep an eye on Sally Janus. She hired you, and then he said to switch over. I'm just doing what I'm told. How about we break clean?"

I let him go. "You can tell Egeleise that Doeppel is dead. They've got the guy who did it."

On the bus out to Rikers, I thought it over. So, Egeleise was in it from the beginning, and he was just using me to find Janus or Doeppel or whatever the hell his name was. I was his puppet, and who knew what he'd done to manipulate me. Was he behind the two hoods in L.A.? Was that a spur to move me forward, to keep me on the case? I didn't know. I'd probably never know. It was ancient history now, just another bizarre turn to an already bizarre case.

At Rikers, they brought in Kenneth Butler. He sat opposite me, a glass partition separating us. We looked at each other for some time without exchanging a word. He was not what I'd expected. For one thing, he was small. Maybe five-six or seven. Thin. Very thin. You could put two fingers around his waist. He had a studious look. The kind of guy you might find hanging around a library, not Times Square. He had a pinched face, close-cropped sandy hair, and a long, thin nose. He wore wire-rimmed glasses. He had a sad, forlorn look about him. His lawyer told me he'd never been in trouble before, that he was "peculiar." I asked what that meant. He said I'd see for myself. He was right.

I said, "Hello." He didn't respond. I looked him in the eye. He didn't blink. I told him my name. It didn't faze him. I asked him if he knew who I was. He didn't answer. I asked him if he knew why he was there. A smile began to cross his face, but before it got far he stopped it. I knew he knew why he was there. I thought maybe I was making some progress, so I asked him where he came from. His lawyer didn't know. No one knew. After I asked him, I didn't either. I asked if he had any family. He didn't answer. Finally, I asked him, "Did you kill Harry Janus?"

For the first time he spoke. "I prefer not to answer that question at this time." His voice was calm, though cold and detached. His mouth moved and the words tumbled out, but there was nothing behind them, no feeling, no sense of understanding. Just words.

"Why did you kill him?"

"I prefer not to answer at this time," he said.

I tried again. "Did someone else kill him?"

"I prefer not to answer at this time."

"Was someone else involved?"

Silence.

There was no point going on. I'd walked in that morning with all kinds of crazy notions. He wasn't guilty. He was a fall guy. Someone had set him up to take the rap. I'd met some powerful men in the last week or so, people who could certainly have arranged to pin a murder on an innocent man. Or maybe they didn't have to. Maybe he was a willing participant in the sham. An insanity plea might get him off. Couple years in an institution and then out on the street to spend any dough he'd be given.

Or maybe he was guilty. A hired killer who got sloppy. And maybe, like Lee Harvey Oswald, he wouldn't even make it to trial. Maybe the conspiracy was so big, so widespread, that I'd never, no matter how long I tried, get to the bottom of it.

That's what I thought going in; it's not what I thought going out. Oh, there was part of me that wanted to believe all that, as much as a kid wants to believe in Santa Claus. But it would have been a lie. Sitting across from Kenneth Butler for even that short a time, I knew. I knew he was the one. I knew he was nutty as a fruitcake. I knew he killed Harry Janus for no better reason than it fit into his deranged scheme of things. Who knew what set him off. Harry Janus walked into that room with a hooker, but he never walked out, and Kenneth Butler was the reason why. It had nothing to do with rock and roll bands, pre-Columbian art, drugs, ancient bones, German and Russian spies, Mexican revolutionaries, assassination plots, wine, women or song. It just happened. And, in the end, did it really matter why? Did it even matter that maybe Harry Janus just got what he deserved? And did it matter if the instrument of his getting his due had nothing whatsoever to do with his past life?

No.

By late that afternoon I was comfortably ensconced back in my regular seat at the Paradise Bar & Grill. I had a little extra money in my pocket and I meant to spend it. I'd worry about the future later…when it didn't matter anymore.

Right then, though, I was the hit of the party. The boys were actually glad to see me. And why not? I was spending money like it was going out of style. I was having such a good time I even let myself get talked into reciting a little po-it-tree. And why not. After all, as someone a lot wiser than me once said, "Life is short, art is long."

Just before I was ready to call it a night, someone popped a quarter into the jukebox and what should come up but a song called "Stomp Out the Fires of My Heart." And you know what, I didn't even give it a second thought. Instead, I just hoisted one in honor of Harry Janus. And the funny thing was, the rest of the boys at the Paradise Bar & Grill did the same.

And they didn't even know him from Adam. ✻